W9-BBZ-446

BRIDGE TO FREEDOM

Isabel R. Marvin

BRIDGE
TO FREEDOM

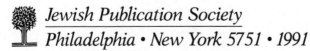
Jewish Publication Society
Philadelphia • New York 5751 • 1991

Library of Congress Cataloging-in-Publication Data
Marvin, Isabel R.
     Bridge to freedom/Isabel R. Marvin.
        p.   cm
     Summary: As World War II winds down, a fifteen-year-old deserter
from the German army reluctantly joins forces with a Jewish girl and
tries to cross the border to safety in Belgium.
   ISBN 0-8276-0377-0 (Cloth)
   ISNB 0-8276-0640-0 (Paperback)
   1. World War, 1939-1945–Juvenile fiction.   [1. World War,
1939-1945–Fiction.   2. Jews–Germany–Fiction]   I. Title.
P27.M3682Br 1991
[Fic]–dc20   90-5103
                                                              CIP
                                                              AC

10 9 8 7 6 5 4 3 2 1

The author acknowledges with love and appreciation the help of her husband David H. Marvin in writing *Bridge to Freedom*. Dave was among the first American troops to cross the Remagen bridge in March, 1945, in the Allies' push toward Berlin at the end of World War II.

All characters are fictitious, except the German officers and non-commissioned officers involved in the effort to destroy the bridge before the Allies took it. All incidents concerning the bridge and its capture, use, and final collapse are true. The *Marshal Cavendish Illustrated Encyclopedia of WWII*, published in England, was a main back-up source of information, along with Ken Hechler's *Bridge at Remagen*.

I.R.M.

EUROPE, 1945. *Darker area denotes German-controlled territory as of March 7.*

1

THE BRIDGE

*T*ucking the package of dynamite inside his jacket, young Kurt Müller began climbing an iron bridge girder. Above his head the railroad bridge stretched from bank to bank across the Rhine River. Already, his fingers were numb from cold. It was an important job, and he hoped he could do his part.

He craned his neck to see the overhead trestles as he made his way toward the main support of the bridge where he planned to place the dynamite. He inched his way hand over hand, legs wrapped around the iron beam, toward the cross section where the girder supported the main structure. That's where the dynamite would do the most damage.

Last night his sergeant had told him what to do. "You're our youngest recruit, Müller, but you're strong and plenty capable of getting up that girder without falling into the river. You take the charge up there and hand the connecting wire to Martin, who'll be on the bridge. He'll attach it to the main cable."

Kurt tried to keep himself from looking down, but

fascination drew his gaze. Seventy meters below his feet, the dark, frigid waters of the Rhine rushed past from south to north. At this stage of the war in 1945, it divided Allied-occupied Germany from the rest of the country. British and American soldiers—the Allied forces—had already taken a wide strip of Germany on the west side of the Rhine. Kurt and the others in his demolition company were there to keep the Allies from crossing the river and marching toward Berlin.

The river was swollen from the spring runoff of ice and snow. Kurt felt an almost uncontrollable urge to jump. He wondered if the human body could survive such a fall.

He slipped suddenly and grabbed at the steel girder, wrapping his legs around it more securely.

"You all right, boy?" Old Martin peered down through the slits between the wooden planks covering the railroad tracks on the bridge. Martin had the easy part of the job. All he had to do was walk out on the bridge and take the wire from Kurt. Earlier they had tried to plant the dynamite from the bridge itself, but it had proved impossible, which accounted for Kurt's dangerous ascent.

"Yes. Don't worry." Kurt reached the underside of the bridge. Feeling inside his jacket for the wire-encircled bundle of dynamite sticks, he stuffed it into one of the metal slots in the girder, which no one had been able to reach from the bridge.

"Here, Martin." He passed the attached wire up through a crack to the old soldier.

Martin reached a gnarled hand for the wire and

hooked it to the main cable, which ran across the bridge into the railway tunnel on the east side of the river. The cable ended in the detonating device. It would not be needed until the enemy was almost upon them.

"Now get down from there before you fall off," Martin growled. "You're making me nervous!"

"I'm okay," Kurt insisted. He turned to look at the tunnel from his perch high on the girder. The Ludendorff Bridge was a railroad crossing with two sets of tracks. Even though Ludendorff was the official name, the soldiers called it the Remagen Bridge because the bridge itself led directly from the town of Remagen on the west bank of the river.

After trains passed over the bridge, they disappeared into the dark mouth of the tunnel on the east side of the river. Kurt couldn't see the tunnel exit.

He wiggled the package of dynamite to make sure it would stay, then climbed back down to the east side of the river and scrambled up the bank. When Martin returned from finishing his part of the wiring, they sat down in the bunker to eat their supper of dry biscuits.

Old Martin grumbled as he ate. "What good will it do to blow up this bridge? The cursed English and Americans will cross the Rhine one way or another. Then it's all over with us. We're beaten, you know."

"Shh! It's bad for morale to talk about losing. That's what Sergeant Faust told us. If anyone should hear you—"

"Oh, you Hitler Youth! All I want to do is go home to my Anna. Did I tell you we have a new grandson?" The old man's face brightened momentarily, then drooped into its habitual careworn lines. "And I don't even know his name. Anna sent word before he was named and there's been no mail since then. What are we doing here, anyway? I'm too old to fight and too old to believe this nonsense any more about Germany winning the war. And you, only fifteen! If Germany had anyone else to fight, they wouldn't have called us up."

Kurt and Martin wrapped themselves in the thin wool blankets from their packs. Even though it was March, the weather was bone-chilling cold. Scattered patches of snow lay like giant footprints upon the earth.

"You told me about your grandson. And I'm not a Hitler Youth and I'm not a Nazi! I know about some of the things the Nazis have done. I could never be the kind of person who knocks on doors in the middle of the night or puts people in jail. I only wanted to be left alone. My parents raised me to think war and fighting are bad. Hitler told all of us we had to fight to save our fatherland from Communism. Wasn't there any other way besides war?"

Martin grimaced. "Too late now. Why didn't you hide back on that farm of yours and stay out of it?"

"My brothers died in the war, and believe me, I wanted to stay on the farm to help my parents. They needed me. But I couldn't say no to the German Army any more than you could. Why didn't *you* hide somewhere?"

"Yes, yes," the old man agreed. "We had no choice."

"Look, I'll take first watch tonight," Kurt suggested. "You take second. We have a big job to do tomorrow. It'll go all right. You'll see. The bridge will blow as planned."

"*You* will see," the old man mumbled, then turned on

his side. He fell asleep almost before the words floated from his vapored breath.

It was so cold Kurt was able to force his eyelids to stay open throughout his watch and halfway into Martin's. If he had been warm and comfortable, he might have fallen asleep immediately. He knew that in each bunker one soldier was keeping watch in case the Americans attacked at night.

Only the rushing water a few hundred meters away interrupted the stillness. The night was quiet and moonless. Kurt tried in vain to make out the silhouette of the bridge. By tomorrow night it would be not be there. He wanted to take one last look. It was difficult for him to realize that soon a famous landmark would be gone. This terrible war was killing Germany and it saddened him.

He woke Martin at 0300 and fell asleep even before the old man stopped complaining.

* * *

Kurt awoke to the sounds of shells exploding. Martin was calmly chewing the crackers that served as breakfast.

"The Americans are firing flares to keep our army from using the bridge to retreat," Martin said. "Don't worry about the damage. The flares explode before they touch the bridge or us. It's from quite a distance, too."

The boy examined the bridge directly in front of them. About a third of the way from each riverbank, a pair of watchtowers stood across from each other like stone sentinels, guarding the bridge from trespassers. Inside, a staircase wound from the ground floor of each tower to the second. Two sets of railroad tracks passed between the towers.

Kurt took a cracker and leaned back. "I don't get it. Why did we waste all that time putting planks across those railroad tracks if we were going to blow the bridge up?"

"We had to cover the tracks so our army could cross them! How else would we get trucks and tanks across this river? You couldn't haul them by train because by now the Americans have destroyed all the trains and a great deal of track on the west side of the river."

"What's actually on that side of the bridge, the west side?" Kurt asked. "I know what's behind us. The tunnel. A cliff. And miles of trees."

"No." Martin crammed another cracker into his mouth, washing it down with coffee he had boiled over the small fire in the bunker. Then he leaned over and spit it on the ground.

"*This* isn't coffee! It stinks! Burned barley, that's what it tastes like. Anna made good coffee, real coffee! No, you don't know what's behind you. The cliffs rise to a height of about two hundred meters."

"I know that."

"What you don't know is that many wine cellars are hidden in these cliffs. Wine-making is a big business in this part of Germany."

"I see." Kurt nodded. "And what's on the other side?" he asked again.

Martin began to kick dirt onto the fire. "Over there is the rest of Germany—the part of our country that the enemy occupies right now—including my home!

There's the road to Bonn, the passage to Luxembourg, Belgium, and France, to freedom from this hell of fighting and losing."

"It isn't freedom for you," Kurt pointed out. "Your home is in Cologne."

"But I go north from Bonn to Cologne. And I will go whenever I get the chance."

They chewed in silence for a moment.

"The Americans are coming, you know," Martin repeated. "The word is the Americans are only about fifty kilometers west of the river! If you could put your ear down by those railroad tracks, you would hear the rumble of their tanks and trucks."

"Why don't we blow the bridge up now — before they get here!"

"Because Hitler is a crazy fool, that's why."

"Don't say that!" Kurt shifted uncomfortably. He looked nervously toward the group of soldiers in the next bunker.

"He is crazy, I tell you." Martin finished his coffee, scowled, and shook out the last few drops. He shoved his canteen into his kit. "Hitler ordered his generals and field marshals to wait to blow the bridges over the Rhine until the very last minute. They will be court-martialed if they disobey and blow them too soon like the Dusseldorf or the Adolph Hitler Bridge at Urdingen. Who do you think would disobey an order like that? A court-martial at this stage of the war means certain death."

Martin wiped his mouth with the back of his hand. "Sometimes I dream of the Kuchen Anna used to make. You should taste her Apfelstrudel!"

Kurt settled back into the bunker. "What will become of us if what you say is true — that we are losing the war?"

Flares began exploding ahead of them, white splashes of fire a few feet above the top of the bridge. Kurt jerked nervously.

"They're coming closer."

"No, no. I told you. They're only trying to keep us from using the bridge."

At that moment, with a loud whistling scream, a shell exploded in the center of the bridge. Kurt leaped to his feet.

"That wasn't a flare! That was an American shell. I know that sound!"

"Yes, yes," the old man agreed. "So they are shelling now. Please excuse me if I don't join the party which begins this afternoon at four o'clock — when we're supposed to blow the bridge. I don't think the bridge will still be here by then. This may be my only chance to get back to Anna and my family!"

With great agility for a man of sixty, Martin scrambled from the bunker and crouching low, began running across the bridge.

"Martin! Wait! Don't go!"

A second later a shell struck directly in front of the old soldier. Before Kurt's horrified eyes, Martin's body flew several feet into the air, then toppled over the side of the bridge into the river.

Kurt knelt in the bunker, which was some protection, and wondered desperately what to do. He sensed that all around him soldiers were leaving the area, running away as Martin had. None of them had tried to cross the bridge, however, which was being showered with exploding shells. It looked as if a hole had opened in the center of the bridge, but Kurt couldn't tell. Probably only the planks were destroyed, not the tracks under them. Martin's sudden death had shocked him into a kind of catatonic state. He could make no decisions for himself. Should he run or should he stay? Without Martin, he felt lost.

Captain Bratge called to the few men who were left. "We're going into the tunnel to detonate the charges," he yelled. "We must blow the bridge. Our radio man reports the Americans are as close as the Becher factory. They'll be here any minute."

Kurt and the other men ran into the tunnel toward the detonating device that stood near the middle. A cable led from it to the sixty charges scattered over the bridge, which would explode when the clocklike key was turned. The men stood helplessly by while the two captains argued about who should give the order. Kurt knew each was afraid to be responsible. Finally Bratge hurried to the front of the tunnel to ask Major Scheller, their recently assigned commander, to do it. Kurt watched the frustrated and angry Bratge plead with Scheller while Captain Friesenhahn stood by the detonator anxiously. Bratge gave up and ran back toward Friesenhahn.

"Blow the bridge!" Bratge yelled. "I'll take the responsibility! Hurry!"

Friesenhahn grasped the key and turned it. The men braced themselves for the explosion. Nothing happened. Kurt held his breath, but only silence filled his ears.

The shell! Kurt thought. The main cable to the detonator is out of commission because it was hit! He felt closed in, as if he were suffocating. Nothing was going as planned. *We'll all be killed by the enemy.*

"Volunteers!" Friesenhahn pleaded. "We need a non-commissioned officer who will set off the emergency charge."

The charge was located immediately beyond the east towers. The man who offered to set it off would be exposed to enemy fire for the brief time it would take him to run out on the bridge. Kurt was only a private, but he wondered if he would be brave enough to volunteer if he were a noncommissioned officer.

Only silence answered the captain's plea. Then stony-faced Sergeant Faust walked up to the captain.

"I'll do it."

"Good!" Friesenhahn exclaimed.

As the men watched, Sergeant Faust crept out of the tunnel entrance in the face of a deadly flurry of American machine-gun bullets. He made a break for the emergency primer seventy meters away. Miraculously, he returned untouched, but there was no immediate explosion.

In panic, Friesenhahn dashed out of the tunnel. He had forgotten the normal delay for the primer cord to burn. With a roar, timbers leaped into the air. The captain ran quickly back to safety.

A hoarse cheer burst from the men, but when the smoke cleared, Kurt saw only slight damage. Americans began crossing the bridge toward them. *Martin was right,* he thought, *the Americans had been coming even as we wired the bridge for destruction. The noise of their trucks and tanks must have echoed down the plank-covered tracks. We actually made the bridge ready for American tanks and trucks!*

Then he saw civilians from the nearby village enter the mouth of the tunnel carrying a white flag. The sound of shelling had convinced them to surrender before the enemy destroyed their homes.

Bratge gathered his men together. "Major Scheller and two other officers have left us. I didn't even see them go," Bratge told them. "We cannot afford to fight any longer. If anybody wants to fight, you may command. That is the new order from the führer."

No one responded.

Bratge squared his shoulders. "I order the fighting to stop. I ask you to lay down your weapons and surrender. According to the rules of war, we must let civilians go first." He nodded toward the group of frightened people who had joined them.

Kurt stood as if rooted to the ground. *Surrender means death,* he thought frantically. *That's what Sergeant Faust told us. I will never see my family again. I'll take my chances in the woods.* He laid his rifle down as ordered.

A few feet in front of Kurt, German soldiers began placing their rifles in a heap at the officers' feet. Some unstrapped handguns to add to the pile. As the men moved forward quietly, not looking at each other, Kurt realized he was behind them, near the tunnel's back exit. Groups of soldiers and civilians milling in front of him would conceal him from the approaching Americans who by now must be halfway across the bridge.

His first backward steps were clumsy and slow. He

thought everyone would turn to look at him as he struggled to breathe quietly and normally. His boots seemed to strike the pebbles underfoot with unusual force. He was sure the noise of his cautious departure would draw all eyes to him. His heart beat loudly, drumming in his ears.

Then he was outside. He knew he couldn't follow the tracks any farther. He would be caught and executed as a deserter by any German unit that captured him. A hill rose above him on the left. Climbing it was his only chance for escape.

His hands and feet became allies, holding on to branches that lashed out at him, finding footholds in the gravel of the cliff. He climbed for what seemed hours, branches clawing at his face. His ascent was almost directionless because of the heavy foliage. He knew he had to stay close to the cliff above the tunnel. Any other path would take him deeper into Germany. On the other hand, the closer he stayed, the more the danger of capture by the Americans.

He stopped to look down and discovered he was high above the front entrance of the tunnel. Before he dodged back into the trees and bushes, he caught a quick glimpse of the scene that swam below him. Sporadic fire burst from the bridge, and he saw German soldiers with their hands linked over their heads marching in front of Americans holding rifles.

He plunged ahead and upward. Tree branches tore at his clothes, took his cap. The thick underbrush of crawling vines and vegetation tripped him several times. Once he stepped into a hole and turned his ankle.

He climbed the cliff, hanging onto anything that would bear his weight. Small rocks scattered and fell under his booted onslaught. Exhaustion was beginning to overtake him when suddenly he tripped and stumbled against the hillside. To his amazement, the ground gave way and allowed him to fall in.

He crashed into semidarkness, slamming hard against the ground inside. He assumed it was a cave since there was no vegetation under his searching hands. It was too dark to tell.

He rolled over on the hard dirt floor and looked up at the sky through the narrow opening. He felt safer inside. He passed his hands over his hips, his ankles. Bruised but no bones broken. Slowly, looking at the clouds drifting by, he began to relax. The war seemed very far away.

Behind him he heard someone breathing.

2

ANOTHER VICTIM OF WAR

Kurt held his breath as long as he could, tensing himself to be ready to dart from the cave if necessary. He listened intently for the sound of breathing again.

He stood slowly and turned cautiously in the direction of the sound. *If I only had my rifle . . . by now it's been tossed into the river. The Americans would make sure no German had access to a weapon.*

As his eyes gradually adapted to the gloom, he saw casks and kegs stacked along the walls and across the back of the cave. *A wine cellar! That's what Martin had said.* He wished desperately for his weapon. *If it's someone with a gun, it's all over. Maybe it's only an animal seeking shelter from the cold March winds.*

He heard a slight rustle as a small figure appeared from between two large kegs. Kurt stepped backward in alarm.

A girl's voice spoke. "I have no weapon and I mean no harm. I was cold. We'll leave your wine cellar as soon as possible."

Kurt tensed. *"We?"* His eyes searched the darkened cave. He saw only one person. She wore a brown school uniform such as some of the girls wore at home in Leipzig. An old tan coat hung over her shoulders.

"It's not my wine cellar," he said. "Even so, I'd like to know what you're doing here." He spoke firmly, hoping to take the upper hand in this strange turn of events.

"If it's not your wine cellar, what are you doing here?" she returned.

"I have as much right as you to be here. Who is with you?"

"No one," she said in a surprised tone.

"You said, 'We will leave.'" He didn't trust her even though she sounded quite young and was obviously German.

"There's just me and a dog that's hurt. I think he's dying."

Kurt's panic began to subside, but he remained watchful, peering into the dark shadows of the cave.

"Where is he?"

"Up by the entrance in the corner." The girl paused. "Are you . . . are you alone?" Her voice quivered.

Kurt could not see her face clearly, but he sensed her fear. She held her hands in front of her as if to ward off a sudden attack. Since he was standing inside the cave entrance in front of the only light source, he wondered if she could really see his face. Perhaps she could see little more than the shape of a man. He stood quietly for a moment, deciding how much to tell her.

Then he said, "There's only me. Show me the dog, please."

She stepped into the center of the cave, and walked to the corner immediately inside the entrance. Now that his eyes had adjusted, he could see a dog lying there motionless.

Kurt walked cautiously to the corner, bracing himself to dart out the cave entrance if confronted. The dog's coat was matted and tangled. Burrs from the underbrush on the hill studded his sides. Kurt knelt and placed his hand on the dog's chest.

"He looks dead."

"I know," the girl said, "but he isn't yet." She knelt beside him. "See, he's still breathing."

Kurt felt it now — short, almost imperceptible motions of the dog's chest. He touched the dog's nose. It was hot and dry. The animal's eyes were closed.

"I think there might be something wrong with his legs," she explained. "He stumbled through the entrance as if he were looking for a place to lie down and die. Animals do that, you know."

"In this light I can't tell," Kurt told her. "Maybe if we move him to the front. It'll soon be dark outside, and I won't be able to examine him."

Together they half lifted, half dragged the large dog to the entrance. In the waning light, Kurt was able to see the girl more clearly. She was small, much shorter than he, but he knew he was tall for fifteen. He thought she was probably close to his age. Her uniform was incredibly dirty and her brown stockings were torn in several places. Her dark hair fell over the collar of her uniform blouse. As she looked from the dog to him, her dark eyes were anxious.

"Can you help him?" she asked softly, pushing the long hair back from her face.

Kurt knew what she was seeing. He had lost his cap in the fight with the underbrush on the hill, and now he ran his hand self-consciously over his blond crew cut. He was aware that he looked like a thousand other blue-eyed soldiers with the same military haircut. Freckles dusted his short, straight nose.

"Why, you're one of the soldiers from the bridge!" she said in surprise. "But you look too young! I thought perhaps you were from the village and that I would be charged with trespassing."

"I'll soon be sixteen," Kurt said stiffly, bending down to the dog. "Let's see, old fellow." Kurt ran his hands slowly over the dog's head, back, shoulders and legs. As he touched the left foreleg, a tremor ran through the animal.

"I think I've found it. Look at his foot." The dog's left front paw was swollen to twice the size of the other feet. Pus oozed from a half-closed wound. "There's something in here," Kurt told her, "and it has to come out."

She murmured, "I should have seen that. Perhaps he was lying on it all this time."

"How long has he been here?" Kurt felt gently along the deep wound.

"Two days," and as Kurt looked at her inquiringly, "I've been here three. I would have left before, but there were so many soldiers on the bridge, and I need to cross it."

"Here it is. A shrapnel fragment. Another victim of war." Kurt grasped the sharp piece of metal and pulled it out as quickly as he could. Whining faintly in pain, the dog raised his head barely an inch from the floor, then with an almost human groan of relief, lowered it.

Dark, almost black blood and pus burst from the open wound. Kurt squeezed the paw tenderly until the discharge slowed to a bright red trickle. He held the paw up from the infected material, which had run onto the cave floor.

"Take the pack off my back. It unbuckles in front," he told the girl. "I don't want his paw to get dirty."

She fumbled with the catch, unfastened it, and laid the pack on the dirt floor.

"Open it and find a small envelope. That's it. It's sulfa powder. Sprinkle it all over his paw while I hold it up."

She tore a corner from the envelope with her teeth, then powdered the dog's foot as Kurt directed.

"Should be bandages in there, too," he said.

Together they wound gauze around the torn foot. Once again they tugged the heavy animal back to the corner. Kurt kicked dirt over the small mound of decaying matter which had gushed from the paw.

"Smells terrible," the girl said. "Does that mean anything?"

"Yes, it may be too late. He could have blood poisoning."

She caught her breath. "I hope not."

"We've done all we can," Kurt told her. "If he shows any sign of life, he'll need water." He looked at her curiously. What in the world was a young schoolgirl doing in a wine cellar? How had she gotten here? Most of all, was she a danger to him? He felt his world had suddenly become amazingly complicated.

Then he asked, "How have you been surviving? I don't see any water here. Only wine casks."

"The snow." She indicated a dipper hanging on one of the keg fronts. "I dig snow out of the deep holes in the woods."

"Go get some now," he ordered, "and we'll put it in my mess kit to melt."

For a moment the girl stared at him with what Kurt interpreted as distrust.

"You know where you've been finding clean snow," he explained. "The dog needs water. What are you afraid of?"

Abruptly she snatched up the dipper. She returned with it full of snow. Kurt unfastened the mess kit handle, which held the two shallow pans together, filled one pan with snow and laid it close to the dog's head.

He patted the dog. "There you are, old fellow. I'll call you Fritz. I had a dog named Fritz once," he said, "but he's . . . gone now."

"Fritz is a good name," the girl agreed. "I was calling him Wolfgang, but I like Fritz better." Then she smiled at the dog and smoothed his fur. It was the first time Kurt had seen her face anything but tense and worried. *Smiling, she's quite pretty*, he thought, *but what's she doing here?* He stood up.

"My name is Kurt Müller, and I — we — were planning to blow up the bridge."

She stood and folded her arms. Then she glared at him

scornfully. "I was watching the *noble* German Army at the bridge, but I didn't know what it was doing there." She sneered. Kurt stared at her.

"I saw the Americans coming long before you and your Nazi friends did! I heard you, yes, you," she said contemptuously as he looked at her in amazement. "I thought you were some man from the village. You were blundering up this hill making enough noise for a whole army." She laughed so bitterly that Kurt stared at her in wonder. "At least," she told him, "you had more sense than they did. You got away. They'll probably get what's coming to them. You do not understand me, I see. Well, fellow refugee, Kurt . . . Müller? I'm Rachel Gildemeister from Berlin. Where are you from?"

Kurt was puzzled by her outburst, but he figured he had as much right to be there as she did.

"My home is, or was, a farm near Leipzig. You've been living and sleeping in this cave for three days?" He looked around at the wine casks, the dirt floor, and the rocks along the cave walls.

"How do you think I got so dirty?" she demanded. She clasped her arms across her stomach suddenly. "I'm starving. I had food, but it's gone. Have you anything to eat? Nazis should be good for something."

Kurt looked at her solemnly. "I'm not a Nazi. I'm only a farmer turned soldier. To be a Nazi you have to be a member of the National Socialist German Workers' Party. My family and I have never been members."

"Never mind that." Rachel waved her hands impatiently. "Do you have anything to eat?"

"I'll check, but it won't be much."

They sat down next to the cave entrance, leaning against an old wooden door that had broken away from its hinges. He searched through his knapsack, setting each item in front of them. It seemed strange to be sharing all his worldly possessions with a total stranger, yet at the moment, no one else knew where he was or cared.

"Blanket, an extra pair of socks. I haven't much left. My canteen, a tin cup, and one box of dry rations!" Triumphantly he pulled out a badly bent cardboard box.

Rachel's hands shook as she extracted each small package from the box. "A can of meat, crackers, and some chocolate! Instant coffee! Cigarettes. Do you smoke?"

"No. They issue those to everybody. Take them."

"I don't smoke either." She put the cigarettes back in the box. "We'll save them in case . . ."

Kurt noticed the "we." She must feel the same as he did, that they were the only two who cared what happened to each other. "In case what?"

"You know, to exchange for a favor. Are you hungry?"

"No," he lied, "but we must be careful. We don't know where the next meal's coming from. Choose something. We'll make the food last until we have a plan."

Rachel's huge black eyes devoured the two small bars of chocolate.

"Eat them," Kurt urged. "I don't like chocolate."

"I don't believe you, but I'm too hungry to argue."

She ripped the foil from the chocolate and ate the candy with little nibbles of pleasure.

Kurt took the dipper outside to look for more snow, then filled up the other side of his mess kit. He sat down in the cave and ate a cracker. The meal with Martin seemed so long ago. So many terrible things had happened since then. Poor Martin. Never saw his new grandchild. Kurt couldn't think about it now.

"Tell me," Rachel said, "have you ever . . . ever killed someone? Shot at the enemy?"

He shook his head. "I've only been in service a couple of months. We — the new recruits — didn't really get any weapons training before we got to the front. If I hadn't used a shotgun on the farm, I wouldn't have been able to handle a rifle. To tell the truth, all we've done is retreat."

He could tell she was trying not to smile.

"I know. Some brave soldier I am."

"What do you think will happen to the rest of your company?" she asked, licking the last bit of chocolate from her fingers.

"The Americans will shoot them all," he said promptly.

"You're afraid of the Americans, but I'm more afraid of the Germans."

"The Germans! You said you were from Berlin. I don't understand."

Rachel looked at him carefully for a moment, searching his young, puzzled face with anxious eyes, then finally said, "I suppose I have to trust you. We're in this together now. I'm a Jew!"

3

AUSCHWITZ

Kurt was astonished. "A Jew!" Almost imperceptibly, he edged away from her shoulder. As the gray twilight faded into night, he could hardly see her face.

"I have nothing against Jews. You're only a schoolgirl. I'd never turn you in or report you. Besides, where would I turn you in? And how? I'd be in as much trouble as you if I tried. My own army would shoot me as a deserter, and the Americans would kill me as one of their enemy."

Rachel laughed. "I know. That's the only reason I dare trust you. Do you know what it means to be a Jew in Germany in 1945? Do you?" she demanded, and when he shook his head, she said, "and don't try to tell me you haven't been told — perhaps even by your parents — that we Jews are unclean or different. I can feel these things."

Kurt felt confused and upset at the turn which the conversation had taken. He didn't hate anybody. What was he supposed to be thinking?

"Rachel, I've lived on our farm all my life, and my

parents aren't political. Most of what I know about the war is what I've been told, that—"

"That you are the master race," Rachel interrupted savagely. "That you are superior Aryans and anyone who is different or not of your *pure* blood is bad and the cause of Germany's problems!"

He felt miserably uncomfortable. "Something like that," he said slowly. "Tell me about your people. Where are your parents?"

"They're dead."

"Dead?"

"My mother, my father,"—she struggled to keep from crying—"and my little brother Kyle."

"When did this happen?" *Maybe this explained her attitude*, he thought. *So much tragedy in the family. Some kind of terrible accident.*

Rachel's voice was harsh as she fought for control. "Sometime before Hanukkah this year, I was coming home from school when I saw an S. S. truck pull up outside our apartment house. I stopped on the corner to watch. I didn't think anyone knew we were Jewish, so it couldn't have anything to do with us. Then somehow I was afraid to go on. Something terrible was happening. They pushed my parents and Kyle into the truck and took them—" Rachel choked and began to sob.

Kurt wished he'd never asked. "Don't tell me if it up-sets you so much."

"No," she sobbed, rubbing her eyes. "I want you to know what your precious führer has done."

Kurt said angrily, "He's not my precious führer! I've told you that. I had nothing to do with this war except

that I couldn't get out of it. Can't you understand that!"
He realized he was shouting at a girl who was openly
crying now.

She swallowed audibly and gained some control over
her quivering voice. "The Nazis killed them!"

"Why would they do that?" He was enormously puzzled. "What happened?"

She tried to calm herself. "We heard that outside of
Auschwitz there is a huge extermination camp for Jews.
And that's where they took them."

"Yes, I've heard of the concentration camps. But—
isn't your family still there?"

"You don't understand!" Tears streamed down her
face. "They're dead. All of them." Sobs shook her body.
"The Nazis have been killing the Jews they took to concentration camps."

He stared at her in amazement. "That's impossible.
Rachel—stop! Are you telling me your family was—. No
human being would simply put another to death without
a trial, without a reason!"

"Oh, no? I can see you don't know what's been going
on. My entire family was killed! I was afraid to go back to
our apartment to get my things, so I went to a friend's
house. I knew her parents were in the Underground.
They're kind people, good friends, and they got news of
my family through the Underground."

He was horrified. *This was unbelievable. How could
his countrymen let the Nazis commit such crimes?* He
didn't know what to say.

"Rachel, how can this be true? Even Nazis wouldn't do
anything like this!"

She looked at him wearily. "No wonder no one helped the Jews. You people didn't know what was happening, and you didn't care."

He was stung by her remark. "I care," he said. "I care about people. And so did my parents. But there was nothing in the papers or on the radio—"

She laughed harshly. "Papers. Radio. Don't you know the Nazis control all of that? People like you hid out on your little farms and let most of us die. How could you not know what was happening?"

He stammered as he said, "I'm sorry, Rachel. To know that you have lost your entire family—there is nothing worse than this!"

Soon her sobbing began to subside. She sniffled as her tears slowed, and he dug into his pocket for a handkerchief.

"This is filthy," he apologized, handing it to her.

She laughed through the tears. "Who cares about clean anymore? I'm lucky to have escaped."

He nodded sympathetically. "Tell me how you got away and how you happen to be here."

"The Underground passed me from house to house. I'm going to try to find my aunt and grandmother in Belgium. That's why I have to cross the bridge. I have a map of the roads on the other side of the river. I'll show it to you tomorrow when it's light." She was finally calm.

"The bridge . . ." he said slowly. "That's impossible. There will be thousands of troops on that bridge night and day. But now we have to sleep."

He covered her with the blanket and then lay down on the other side of the cave under his jacket. He was disturbed by what she had told him. *Was it true?* He simply could not accept her story. *How could Nazis be so inhuman? She would find her family someday.* Yet he wondered. She had been so sure.

He thought about it for a few minutes. If he had come upon someone loading his family into an S. S. truck, he would have . . . would have . . . run away, the same as she had. *What could one person do to save them?* He sighed. He was so tired. Too much had happened today. He could no longer absorb it all.

Rachel must have been exhausted from her crying because soon her breathing became slow and regular. Kurt fell asleep shortly, but a sound in the cave awakened him a few hours later. He heard a clumsy *lop, lop* as Fritz drank a few sips of water. Kurt smiled to himself in relief. The next thing he knew, morning light poured into the cave.

4

A REFUGE AND A TRAP

*S*tretching his arms over his head, Kurt stood up slowly and yawned. Every muscle ached. *First the fall into the wine cellar. Then a night spent lying on a cold, dirt floor. It isn't much worse than the bunker,* he thought, *but the dirt was loose and softer there.*

He went outside to check on the bridge traffic. As he suspected, hundreds of Allied troops streamed across the bridge. Traffic went only one way: east. He watched the soldiers and vehicles come toward him, then disappear into the tunnel under the hill. No sign of any prison compound. He supposed the prisoners had all been shot. He ducked his head to reenter the cave. Fritz lay very still in the corner, but his breathing was slower now and visibly expanded his rib cage.

"Hello, Fritz." Kurt leaned over to pat the sleeping animal's head. The dog's eyes did not open, but his long plumed tail flopped feebly, then relaxed. The water in the pan was gone. Kurt looked down at Rachel, curled up tightly in the blanket. Her long dark lashes rested on white cheeks, and her hands were clenched even in sleep. He picked up the dog's empty pan and went outside to look for a pocket of snow. The snow would be gone soon. What would they do for water then? They didn't dare go down to the river.

He found a small snowdrift on the far side of a fallen log and scraped away the gray top layer. Then he dipped the pan in to fill it.

When he returned, Rachel was spreading the blanket on the floor. She kept her eyes lowered shyly as she said, "I'll go outside and wash my face with snow. I must look a mess."

Kurt felt odd. He had never been around girls much except at school. Of course, there was Katzi, his little sister, but she was only seven. *And here I am,* he thought, *living in a cave with a girl my own age!* Somehow the situation they found themselves in had made them instant friends. Or if not exactly friends, at least allies. But her attitude toward the German people both puzzled and alarmed him. He wondered if he should trust her completely. Now that he was a deserter, he must be careful.

Rachel's cheeks were glowing when she reentered the cave. He was ashamed of himself for thinking she was not to be trusted. They sat down cross-legged on the blanket to divide the food.

"One cracker for you," Kurt alloted, "one for me, and one for Fritz when he wakes up."

"Fritz!" Rachel cried out. "I forgot about him." She hurried to the dog and stroked his matted coat. "There, there, Fritzie. How's my doggie?" Fritz opened his eyes and began struggling to his feet.

"Look, look, Kurt! He's going to live," she said in wonder. "I think he wants to go out!"

Kurt put his arms around the dog's chest and helped Fritz wobble three-legged out of the wine cellar. The dog leaned weakly against a tree and after several false starts, held up one leg. Then favoring the bandaged foot, he stumbled clumsily back into the cave corner, lapped at the melting snow with a long pink tongue, and flopped down with a huge sigh.

"I think he's going to be all right," Kurt said proudly.

"You did it!" She clapped her hands. "We did it. I'm so glad!"

They sat down again to divide the food. Kurt opened the tiny can of meat with its attached key and divided the little sausages equally. They ate the small portions of food slowly, relishing each mouthful. Kurt fed Fritz two tiny pieces of meat and a cracker. Fritz ate them quickly and stared at Kurt expectantly.

"He's hungry, too. We'll have to do something about food. This cave may be a refuge, but it's also a trap. I don't dare leave, and we can't stay without food," Kurt said.

She nodded. "We need food all right. But Fritz can't walk well enough yet for me to leave."

"If he could walk, where would you go?"

"To Belgium," Rachel announced triumphantly. "Right across that bridge!"

"I wonder if I could get across the bridge without being captured," Kurt said. "I can't stay here."

"Come with me," she said abruptly. "Even if you're German, two can plan better than one."

He looked at her for a moment. It was an impossible idea. They would never get across the bridge without being seen. But he couldn't stay here forever. And he couldn't go home.

"Maybe," he said. "I don't know what else to do."

Suddenly they heard faint shouting from below. They ran outside to investigate. A huge tank destroyer had broken partially through the temporary bridge planking and turned sideways on the bridge, blocking all traffic behind it.

Swaying dangerously, it hung out over the Rhine River. As they watched, groups of soldiers attempted to free the destroyer. When that didn't work, they tried to push it over the side.

Fascinated by the tense, almost soundless struggle below, the two sat down under a fir tree to watch. A driver occasionally attempted to maneuver the great machine either forward or back. Workers crawled about on the bridge flooring, trying to rebuild the planking. Within the hour, the huge mechanical monster was backed slowly off the bridge to the sound of faint cheers. The flow of traffic resumed. Rachel studied the bridge, elbows on her knees, hands cradling her chin.

"The Americans are coming across the bridge toward us. They seem to disappear at this end. I can't see over the crest of the hill."

"The bridge was for trains until we laid planks across the two sets of railroad tracks," Kurt explained. "The tracks lead into a tunnel under this hill. That's how I got away yesterday. I slipped out the back end of the tunnel and circled around to climb this cliff."

"Then where do the tracks go?"

"I think the Americans will follow them for about six-teen kilometers to the Autobahn — best highway in Germany," he added bitterly.

"Then where?"

"I don't know. Maybe to Frankfurt. No one who isn't part of the Allied forces can cross that bridge with all those soldiers and trucks on it," Kurt said firmly. "You and I haven't a prayer of getting across."

She nodded, but he could see her mind considering the possibilities. "What are we going to do about food? Thinking about it makes me hungry again."

"There's a small village below us and to the right through the woods. Sergeant Faust told us all about this area the first night we camped here. The people of the village surrendered to the Allies at the bridge right before I . . . left. To reach it, we have to go behind the cave and down through the thickest part of the forest so we can't be seen," Kurt told her.

"I know. I came through it to get here. By now most of the townspeople will have run away. You can't go in that uniform!"

Kurt shrugged and spread his hands. "You're right, but a *girl* can't walk two kilometers through dense woods into a village alone to buy food — or steal it! I have only a few marks. Even if you had plenty of money, you couldn't do it. What can a *girl* do in such a situation?"

Rachel stood angrily. "I can do it better than you can! How do you think I got here from Berlin?" She tossed her dark hair. "Watch me!" She glared at him.

He stood up also. "One of us must go. On that I agree. But please be careful," he warned.

Her face relaxed. "Of course I'll be careful. I don't want to get caught any more than you do." She looked down at herself. "I should try to make myself more presentable. Look at my stockings!"

She held up one leg in its tattered hose for his inspection. "The townspeople mustn't think me a refugee. I should look as if I belonged there. I had a change of clothes in a bag, but I had to leave the last Underground house in such a hurry I left everything behind."

"I think Sergeant Faust said the village is called Erpel, but I'm not sure," Kurt said.

"Yes, it is. I'll get ready."

In a few minutes she returned. She had evidently combed her hair. She wore the tan coat. As she tied a black knitted scarf loosely over her head, she looked at him for approval.

"Finished," she said. "Will I pass?"

"My inspection, yes." He handed her what little money he had. "You will be careful?"

"Naturally. You aren't worried that I might turn you in?"

They stood looking at each other for a long moment. Then Kurt said quietly, "You wouldn't do that to me."

She said nothing for a few seconds. "No, I wouldn't. You're right about that. I like having someone to talk to, someone who shares my problems. Right now we need each other, but I warn you that if I have to make a choice, I intend to save myself."

He nodded. "I can understand that. That's what I was doing when I ran away from the bridge."

"And anyway," she said and laughed, "if I turned you

in, I'd have to admit trespassing in their stupid old wine cellar! There's also the strong possibility that a reward-hungry resident would tell the Americans where we are hiding. Auf Wiedersehen!"

She began walking toward the trees behind the cave. When she reached the line of tall pines, she turned and waved. He returned her wave without smiling. As he watched, she disappeared into the woods. He wondered if he should be afraid for himself. All his life he had relied on his instincts about people. Was he wrong about her?

5

A LOAF OF BREAD

*A*fter Rachel entered the woods she looked back again, but she could no longer see Kurt. As soon as the branches closed around her, it was as if she were in another land. Her heart pounded, and she fought to keep herself calm.

I should stay near the side of the hill, she thought, *close enough to catch a glimpse of the village now and then but not close enough to be seen from the bridge. I'd probably be shot by the Americans as a spy if they caught me. And if the villagers knew I was a Jew, they might report me.*

She pushed her way through the trees. Thorny bushes clutched at her coat and stockings. Low-hanging branches grabbed the black knitted scarf. She stopped to untangle it, then put it around her neck under her coat.

Several times branches slapped her unexpectedly in the face. She occasionally scrambled through the trees to spot the village. She found herself counting trees, then her own footsteps. *How alone I am! Until Kurt came, I didn't know how much I needed to talk to someone — even a German soldier!*

The woods were dense. She felt as if she were the only one ever to walk here. *There must be a path to our wine cellar,* she thought. *People have been on this slope before if they've built wine cellars here.*

She had seen more than one cellar when she first came up the hill, but except for hers, they had all been heavily padlocked. She decided the paths must lead over the open side of the cliff where she would be seen walking. She lowered her head and held her arms ahead of herself to protect her face from thick branches.

The forest began to thin gradually as she neared the village. ERPEL, a small sign proclaimed above a deserted tannery at the edge of the woods. A faint odor of rotting animal hides leaked from the boarded-up door. She sat down on the steps of the shop and removed her torn stockings. Her legs were cold without them, but she had decided the stockings were too ragged. Removing her money first, she wadded up the stockings and pushed them down into her right coat pocket. After she counted the few marks, she stuffed the money alongside the stockings. She wondered briefly if that really was the only money Kurt had. *It must be,* she decided. *What good would money do him if he couldn't go into a store?*

She walked down the road leading to the center of the village with her hands clenched in her pockets. She assumed a casual air as if she lived there and was intent on an errand. Many of the houses appeared abandoned, and several shops were boarded shut. She passed a yard where a middle-aged woman was hanging clothes on a line although the clothing froze stiff in seconds. The woman looked at her curiously.

The villagers probably know everyone who lives in this town, Rachel thought grimly. She nodded politely to the woman and continued walking. She came finally to a small shop with a ham hanging in the window.

Rachel entered the store and walked to the counter. The burly man behind it was weighing beans for an elderly lady dressed in black. Turning away so the proprietor could not see into the purse, the woman opened her tiny snap purse and removed the money.

"Twenty Pfennigs!" she snorted, and slapped the coins on the counter. "The beans will be full of little stones when I get them home, Mr. Kronstadt. They always are." She snatched up the small bag and flounced to the door. "I would buy a bit of ham hock to go with them, but you would charge me triple! Ach, such times we live in."

"Yes, ma'am," the man said wearily. "Can I help you, young lady?"

Rachel looked through the glass counter on her left. The counter was only half full of meat, but her mouth watered so much she thought the man must be able to see it. She swallowed.

"A piece of that cheese." She pointed it out. "Four marks' worth, please."

When he cut the piece of cheese and placed it on the scale, her heart sank. It was so small.

"And a box of matches, too."

"Will that be all?"

She nodded faintly, picked up the cheese and matches and left. She wandered down the street, looking in the windows, fingering the money in her pocket nervously. She passed a women's clothing store. LATEST FASHIONS.

She saw only one clothes rack. Hanging on it were German Army jackets of varying sizes.

Next to the clothing store stood a bakery, and Rachel pressed her face hard against the cold glass, staring at the meager display. A huge tray of round hard rolls dominated the shelf. Beside it sat several loaves of bread, some oblong, others round. An elaborately decorated white cake fed her hungry eyes until she realized it was made of cardboard. *Even a baker couldn't get that much sugar!*

She squeezed the money in her pocket. *Probably not enough for a big loaf. Maybe I'll come back and get a few rolls. I had better see the rest of the shops first.* She moved on reluctantly.

Across the street was a small railway station, deserted except for a small dog trotting from one four-foot post to another, sniffing busily.

She turned the corner. Coming toward her was an elderly fat woman whose stomach protruded through her unbuttoned army jacket. She spoke rapidly to the man with her although she did not look at him. Limping beside her, the gray-haired man also wore an army jacket. He hobbled along, fingering his mustache and gazing into shop windows. As the couple approached Rachel, they passed a small saloon.

Quietly and without a sign to the talking woman, the old man disappeared into the darkened interior of the bar. Still talking loudly, the woman waddled past the girl. Rachel smiled to herself. A stale beer odor assaulted her nostrils as she passed the tavern.

She turned the corner again. A bicyclist with a large

wicker basket strapped to the back fender rode down the street toward her. Long loaves of bakery bread filled his basket. The rider was young and whistled merrily as he peddled down the street.

When he turned the corner, the bicycle hit a hole in the street causing the basket to sway precariously. He jerked the bike forcibly to keep it upright, and one of the loaves sailed out in an arcing dive behind him into the bushes.

Rachel held her breath. The boy's whistle faded as he continued down the street toward the bakery. She looked around. A woman shaking a dust mop from a second-story window gave her what Rachel interpreted as a disapproving look, then slammed the window.

Rachel walked quickly to the bush. She glanced at the buildings close to her. No one was watching as far as she could tell. Bending down, she groped under the bush and came up with the glorious loaf of bread. She held it to her face for a second to inhale the wonderful fresh-baked aroma. Then she placed it under her arm and walked slowly in the direction of the hill. *Don't run,* she told herself.

"Oh, Fraülein, Fraülein," a voice called from above. Rachel began to walk a little faster. She knew a stranger running through the streets of a small village would draw immediate attention. "Miss, miss — wait!" Rachel looked up. The woman who had shaken the dust mop had opened the window and stuck her head out. An old man came toward Rachel from the corner store.

"Stop that girl, Herr Volkman!" the woman called to him. "Make her wait till I come down!"

The old man lifted his cap politely and said hesitantly, "Frau Leibenstein wishes to speak with you, Fraülein."

As she stood reluctantly on the edge of the walk, he went slowly past her, stumping along with the aid of a short cane. He stabbed the cane vigorously into the low bushes on either side of the walk until the object of his search—a small, sniffing terrier—emerged. The little dog whisked rapidly between the old man and his stick, almost upsetting his master, and vanished into the brush on the opposite side of the path.

"Darn pup, how many times have I told you not to . . ." The old man stumped on down the street.

Rachel was afraid to run. *So many people only a shout away,* she thought.

The woman who had called hurried from the front door of her house. "Fraülein, I *must* speak with you!"

She saw me take the bread! Rachel clutched the loaf. *I probably don't have enough money left to pay for a big loaf like this. I'll have to give it back.*

"Yes?"

"You are not from our village," the woman stated.

"No, not exactly. I had to go to the store for—"

The woman interrupted, "Aren't you Frau Hauptmeir's granddaughter from Cologne?"

"Who?" Rachel stalled for time to consider her answer.

"I know you are a stranger here. Are you Frau Hauptmeir's granddaughter?"

"Why, uh, yes."

"I knew it! She is worse. Why else would they have sent for you?"

"No, no," Rachel answered hastily. "She isn't worse, but she can't have visitors yet. I must hurry with the shopping for our meal."

"Of course, dear." Frau Leibenstein beamed. "And tell her I would know you anywhere, child. The same big brown eyes as your mother! Run along now. Remind your Grossmutter we are thinking of her."

"Certainly," Rachel said and hurried away with the wonderful loaf under her arm.

She made one more stop before she headed back to the tannery. She knew her conscience would bother her about her last errand, but she felt the end result justified the means. As she started up the hill again, her empty stomach growled. She was so hungry she felt weak. Perhaps a small nibble of the cheese . . .

She knelt as soon as she was out of sight among the trees and unrolled the paper containing the piece of cheese. Then she looked at it for a few seconds. It was so small! A hungry person could eat the whole thing and not be full. She thought about Kurt waiting — and Fritz. Fritz must be almost starving by now. While he had been ill, food for him hadn't been a problem. Now . . .

She rolled up the cheese again and put it in her pocket. There were three mouths to think of now, not merely her own selfish hunger. The climb back to the cave seemed endless as she held the delicious-smelling fresh bread close in her arms.

6

SOLDIERS FIND THE CAVE

*A*t the cave, Kurt watched the bridge activity periodically as he paced back and forth in the small meadow in front of the wine cellar. He was careful to keep well back from the cliff's edge.

Fritz awoke and tore at the bandages with his teeth, worrying and nibbling at the gauze as he lay in the sun.

"Let's see, boy." Kurt carefully unwound the soiled bandage. He examined the wound. It was pink and raw looking, but no new infection had formed. Now that the dog was alert, Kurt knew he would tear off any new bandage.

Some change in the atmosphere, a far-off, barely audible sound, alerted Kurt. He leaned over Fritz and covered the dog's muzzle with his hand.

"Quiet, Fritz, quiet!" he whispered into the dog's silken ear. Then he crawled to the edge of the cliff in front of the wine cellar. *Soldiers! A good commander would order his troops to search the area.*

Below him he saw a squad of soldiers, eight men, fanning out from the bridge level and slowly climbing the hill, rifles held at the ready. He crawled backwards until he was away from the edge of the hill, then darted into the cave, tossed the utensils into his pack and ran back to Fritz. He helped the dog to his feet.

"Come on, Fritz," Kurt whispered. "Hurry."

The dog limped along slowly, holding up the injured paw and looking trustingly at the boy. The two made their way slowly to the left side of the clearing where Kurt coaxed the dog to lie down behind a huge fallen tree.

Bushes obscured Kurt's vision, but soon he heard the footsteps of the American soldiers as they reached the top of the cliff. The boy lay flat against the damp earth. He heard faint laughter from the soldiers after they entered the cave.

They've discovered the wine casks, he thought grimly. *They'll return and bring more troops with them.*

He gripped Fritz hard, willing him to be silent. He felt the dog's strong heart thudding inside the deep chest wall, and he sensed the intensity of Fritz's silent listening. The dog did not move or bark.

After an eternity of fearful waiting, the footsteps and voices were gone. Kurt lay still as long as he could stand it, then speaking softly to Fritz, began to walk quietly back to the cave, pausing often to listen. The two went inside hesitatingly. *Empty!* Fritz heaved a sigh and sank on his side, once again nibbling at his injured paw.

On an impulse, Kurt searched the cave several minutes for an instrument of some kind to puncture one of the kegs. It should be here. They would want to test the wine from time to time. Finally he found the faucet tap on the ground under a cask. He removed his boot and pounded the tap into a small keg with his boot heel. Then he held his mess-kit cup up to the drain and turned the rusty tap handle. The wine began to trickle into the cup and when it was full, he released the handle.

He leaned down, stroking the dog gently with his left hand. Fritz was methodically and unhurriedly licking his sore paw.

"That a boy, Fritzie, you're the best doctor. Pretty soon you can take care of yourself." He pushed the dog's head tenderly away from the paw and poured wine over the wound.

"That's the only disinfectant I have, my friend. We have to keep that foot clean a little longer."

Kurt sat back on his heels, watching the dog begin to lick again but faster and with more interest. Fritz was a large dog with shaggy red hair and a plumelike tail. His ears were long and must have been silken once. Kurt had no idea what kind of dog he was.

He pulled burrs from the dog's coat and rubbed at dried mud wherever he found it. He tried to comb the long, tangled hair with his fingers. Suddenly he heard a crunching sound from the underbrush outside the cave.

He rose and went cautiously to the wall by the cave entrance. If the soldiers had come back, it was too late to escape. Waiting with tensed muscles, he stood silently inside the entrance with his back to the wall.

When a dark figure entered the cave, Kurt reached one arm around the intruder's neck and pulled back sharply. The body was slight, and then he recognized Rachel's hair against his face. He released her.

"Sorry," he panted. "Don't ever jump through this entrance again. I could have hurt you."

She gasped for a moment. "It's only me! Were you scared?"

"Yes," Kurt admitted, "and it's best for both of us to stay afraid. While you were gone, enemy soldiers searched the cave. Fritz and I hid outside. They found the wine, so they'll be back. You shouldn't come bursting in here."

"Are you and Fritz all right?" she asked anxiously. When he nodded, she held up the long loaf of bread and the package of cheese and matches. "See what I have. Such bounty!"

"Ahh." Kurt admired the bread. "You've done well. Did you buy it or steal it?" He accepted the loaf.

She laughed. "That's a long story. Look what else!" She placed the cheese and matches on top of a cask and reached one hand into each of her coat pockets and brought forth triumphantly a long brown cotton stocking in each hand.

"They're somewhat damp, but they'll dry." She laughed again at his surprised expression. "I took them from a convenient clothesline right before I left the village." She draped the stockings over a nearby cask so that the greater part of them dangled free. "I needed them." She shrugged. "First things I ever stole. My mother didn't raise a thief, but—"

"It adds a little touch of home," Kurt joked, "to have ladies' stockings drying on the furniture."

"You didn't know I had relatives in Erpel, did you?" And as his mouth fell open in surprise, she chuckled. "I turned out to be Frau Hauptmeir's granddaughter from Cologne." Then she told him about the mistaken identity and the lucky bread accident.

"You're a quick thinker, Rachel. If someone confronted me, I wouldn't be able to think of anything to say."

She nodded. "You mean I've turned into a liar! And a thief," she said forlornly.

"Surviving," he reminded her. "That's what we're doing."

From the corner Fritz thumped his tail for Rachel's attention. She hurried over to pet him. "Oh, Fritz looks better! But why does his foot smell so funny? Is it blood poisoning?"

Kurt laughed. "No, it's wine! You cut the bread and cheese, and I'll add wine to our feast."

He jumped to his feet and held the tin cup again to the drain, twisting the rusty tap handle with great force.

Rachel laid the bread and cheese on the blanket between them. "Wine?" She was amazed. "How?"

Kurt explained to her the procedure of tapping the wine kegs, adding that his father had once made wine on the farm. They handed the cup back and forth. It was the only one they had.

"See." Kurt pointed to the dog. "Even Fritz likes the wine."

She smiled. "Nineteen forty-five is a good year for wine."

"This wine could have been here for years," Kurt told her. "There's no way of knowing. We must be careful. We need clear heads."

"You're always so serious! What did you do for fun back on the farm, Kurt?"

"Oh, we had a saddle horse. I loved to ride. I always wished for a bicycle, though."

"*I* had a bicycle and wanted a horse!" She grinned at him.

Fritz raised his head from his paw and began growling.

Rachel was startled. "What's the matter with him?"

Slowly gliding into their consciousness came a faint roaring sound, which gradually grew louder.

Kurt listened intently, then cried, "Planes! German bombers!"

7

LEIPZIG

*K*urt reached quickly for his pack, shoved everything into it, and slipped the straps over his shoulders.

"What are you doing?" Rachel asked anxiously.

"We could be buried alive here. Hurry!" Kurt removed his belt and fastened it around Fritz's neck as a leash. Then the three moved as quickly as they could through the cave entrance into the tall pine trees to their left. Fritz' progress was halting, and Kurt scooped him up in his left arm. He grabbed Rachel's hand and they scrambled for the shelter of the trees.

Flinging themselves on the ground, they overlooked the bridge. Fritz lay between them, big head on his paws, back legs stretched out behind him. The noise of the bombers ground in their ears, almost too loud to hear each other's voices. Fritz whined as the sound accelerated. Kurt threw one arm over the dog's back.

"Easy, Fritz, easy," he consoled.

Below them the Americans scurried frantically to position the antiaircraft guns, which Kurt recalled his unit had left behind at the tunnel's entrance. As the bombers approached the bridge, the soldiers below began firing. The *ack-ack* sound of their fire punctuated the roar of the planes.

"It's like enormous orange flowers in a fireworks' display," Rachel said as she lay on her stomach with her elbows on the ground, hands cradling her chin.

"The flak? Orange flowers?" Kurt's mind groped for the nagging memory of a training film. *Orange?*

Rachel covered her head with her arms as the planes released their bombs. They exploded near the bridge, most of them slightly above the water.

Kurt thought one might have made a direct hit on a lower support of the bridge. Abruptly the noise of the bombs ceased as the planes circled for another run at the bridge. For a few minutes the two observed the continuing orange ground fire bursting below them. Suddenly the ten planes veered to the west and flew off without dropping any more bombs.

Kurt sat up in surprise. "What happened? There are only a few guns on this side of the bridge. We didn't have time to bring more across. How could this small amount of antiaircraft fire scare off the bombers? They'll be back. We can count on that. We have to get out of here, but where do we go?"

Rachel looked at him curiously. "*We?* Don't you want to go home? You must know Germany has all but lost the war. It'll soon be over. All you have to do is hide out until it's safe and then go home."

Kurt looked down at Fritz and rubbed the dog's back slowly as he answered. "I can't go home."

"Why?"

"Because home isn't there anymore." He hid his face in the dog's soft hair. "Anyway, it could be months before it's safe to wander around Germany again — a free person. Especially," he added bitterly, "in a German uniform."

Rachel started to speak, then shivered. "It's getting cold, and I think rain is starting. Do we dare risk a fire? We have matches now."

Kurt told her smoke probably wouldn't be noticed amid the confusion of bombers, antiaircraft fire, and troop movements. They gathered sticks in the growing darkness, a huge pile of them. Even Fritz tried to carry a stick to them in his mouth. When Rachel held out her hand, the dog limped slowly to her and placed the stick carefully into her outstretched hand.

"Look at him." She laughed. "He thinks he's a retriever."

"I think he's a smart dog," Kurt said seriously. "Let's see what he knows."

He walked slowly across the stretch of ground in front of the wine cellar. "Here, boy, here, Fritz."

The animal looked at him questioningly, then hobbled toward him, looking up and wagging his tail. Kurt whistled softly to the dog and began walking. Fritz limped slowly beside him, looking up, waiting for the next command.

Without glancing at the dog, Kurt said firmly, "Heel, Fritz, heel!"

Fritz dropped behind Kurt immediately and followed him a few more halting steps, which brought them both up against a big tree.

"Sit, Fritz, sit!" Kurt commanded. The big dog hesitated a second, then sat, gazing anxiously up at Kurt.

The boy called softly back to the amazed girl. "Look at this! Isn't he a fine dog? Watch."

He looked down at Fritz and said sharply, "Stay, Fritz, stay!" Then Kurt walked slowly away.

Although Fritz appeared anxious, he remained in the sitting position for a few seconds, then got up, turned nervously around and sat down again, watching Kurt frantically.

Kurt clapped briskly. "All right, boy, come, Fritz." The dog plodded slowly to him, making an effort to put some weight on his injured foot. Kurt stooped and hugged him heartily, stroking the beautiful head.

Rachel was astonished. "How did you teach him all that?"

Kurt continued to pet the dog. "Someone else did. I taught him nothing. He's a well-trained dog, and he's going to be all right."

"But how did you know?"

"I didn't, for certain. When he carried the stick and gave it to you, I was curious. My brother Josef and I trained our Fritz, and I thought maybe someone had worked with this dog. And they have! He's a wonderful dog."

They carried the sticks into the cave and laid them down in front of the doorway. Kurt ceremoniously lit the stack. Presently the fire crackled and snapped. The smoke rose to the cave ceiling, then filtered slowly out the entrance. They spread the blanket near the fire and sat down.

"Tell me about your home," Rachel prompted.

"We had a nice farm," Kurt began. "A big coal stove in the kitchen. The fire made me think of it. Mother always had me bring her kindling, mostly corncobs. She used to repeat a story often, something I once said: 'I wish we could say it like in the Bible—*let there be corn cobs*—and there would be corn cobs!' I hated picking them up from the pigsty."

Rachel laughed. "You wanted your own little miracle."

"Yes, but I was only seven years old then. We milked twelve cows, usually, and raised twice as many pigs. We had a big vegetable garden. With all that, we hardly needed to buy anything. Just sugar and coffee, things like that."

"Did you have fruit trees?" She lay back on the blanket, firelight reflecting in her dark eyes. She folded her hands on her stomach. "Or chickens?"

"Apple trees and plum. Mother always made jelly from the fruit. And we had chickens." Kurt lay back also, stretching his long arms over his head to scratch Fritz's hide. The dog responded with a groan of pleasure.

"Do you have brothers and sisters?"

"I did." He was silent a few seconds. "Josef went down in a U-boat in the English Channel. He was my closest brother. My oldest brother, Hans, never came back from Minsk on the Russian front in 1941. I have a little sister, Katzi, but I don't know where she is."

Rachel was silent. The firelight played on her hair and skin. She might have been asleep for all he knew. They lay there quietly in the warm cave. She spoke without opening her eyes.

"Your parents?"

"Our farm is close to the aircraft plant at Leipzig — which was blasted in February." He cleared his throat to keep his voice from breaking. "My family escaped. That's all I know. I don't know where they are. The farm — everything — gone!"

"I'm sorry," she finally said. "Someday you'll find them. When it's safe to search, you can go back."

"I know. If I live, I will."

"Go to sleep now," she said. "Tomorrow will be better. Tomorrow I'll show you the map. We'll make a plan. That is, if you want to try crossing the bridge."

Kurt watched the flickering flames. The dancing fire threw monstrous shadows on the wine cellar walls. He shrugged helplessly. "I can't stay here."

After she fell asleep, he began thinking of the farm. Often at night when he had first been called into the army, he had wished he could sleep again under the patchwork quilt his grandmother had sewn so painstakingly for him before the cataracts had clouded her poor old eyes.

The quilt had patches from all the dresses he ever remembered his mother and sister wearing. Squares from the pink-flowered dress his mother used to wear to church on Sunday. The checked square, a leftover piece from Katzi's blue dress for the first day of school. He had taken her by the hand up to the classroom door and pressed the small trembling hand into the teacher's.

"This is my sister Katzi, Frau Bromlen. She is a little frightened, I think."

Frau Bromlen stroked the child's hand and boomed in her familiar, hearty way, "Come, come, little Katzi. I did not eat your brothers, and I will not eat you. Let's find the right desk for you beside Helga, who will be your good friend soon. My, what a pretty dress! Did your mother make it?"

Katzi nodded and pulled back to fling her arms around Kurt's long legs.

"You'll be there when I get home, Kurt? Don't go away to the army! I'm afraid you'll never come back. Just like Josef and Hans!" She was crying again.

Kurt knelt beside her, trying to disengage the thin arms. "Don't cry, Katzi. You promised me this morning. No tears. Don't worry. I'm only thirteen and the fürher doesn't want babies like me. I won't go anywhere."

But a year and a half later, he had to break his promise to Katzi because all the older able-bodied German men had already been conscripted. His mother did not cry when the notice came, but her face was like marble. She gave him six pairs of woolen socks.

"Remember, keep your feet dry so they won't freeze. If you can't keep them dry, rub them often," was all she said.

And his father. He had never seen his father cry before. He pushed the memories away again. It hurt too much to remember. *Tomorrow we'll make a plan. We must. The farm is gone.*

8

ORANGE FLOWERS BLOOM AGAIN

*J*ust before dawn, the planes returned. The three refugees hurried out of the wine cellar, but Rachel pouted. "I'd rather be safe here in the cave than out there in the cold rain."

"I wouldn't," Kurt said firmly. "I have a great fear of being trapped inside a small place. Come on."

Kurt wrapped the blanket around Rachel and himself to keep off the misty drizzle. Fritz huddled between them, whining at the roar of the plane engines and the occasional whistle of a bomb falling toward the bridge.

Below them in a flurry of activity, the flak guns fired again and again, puffs of orange phosphorescent smoke squirting at timed intervals, showering the gray sky with sparks and echoing back from the cliff in sharp bursts of sound.

"That's what's wrong!" Kurt shouted. "Orange. They're orange."

"What did you say? There's so much noise."

Kurt put his mouth up to her ear. "The Americans down there are firing our antiaircraft guns, the ones we left. It makes Luftwaffe bomber pilots think we still have the bridge! They get orders to bomb the bridge at Remagen to keep the enemy from using it, and when they get here, it looks as if it's still under German control. I bet they wonder why we're shooting at them. Look. Now they're leaving."

Rachel looked puzzled.

"Don't you understand? We left the guns all set up on the east bank. We were surprised by the enemy before we could move them. The Americans didn't have time to bring their own guns across, so they're firing ours. It's keeping our bombers from coming back to finish off the bridge!" He shook his head. "Martin often said there was lots of confusion in combat. The bomber pilots must think the gunners can't identify the planes in the dark and rain."

"How do you know that's what's happening?"

"I finally remembered a training film. American antiaircraft fire is white—like lightning. Ours is not. When you said 'orange flowers,' I started thinking."

The sky began to lighten. Now that the planes were gone, traffic moved again on the bridge. Kurt pointed to the river.

"See? Pretty soon it won't matter if bombers blow up the Remagen Bridge. The Americans have almost finished a bridge on either side of it. Over there"—he pointed right—"is a pontoon bridge. On the left, about two kilometers down the river, a big treadway bridge. Soon they won't need the main one."

"What are they doing to the sides of the bridge?" Rachel asked.

Kurt examined the bridge. Several soldiers were stringing wire wrapped with white tape on the driver's side between the walkway and the bridge itself.

"With this rain, it'll be very dark at night and they drive without lights. The white tape will help the drivers find their way. If they go too far to either side, they'll hit a railing. The tape should help keep them on course."

Rachel shivered. "Let's get inside," she begged. When they returned to the cave, they built up the fire again and made hot coffee for breakfast. Kurt drank from the mess cup, Rachel from the dipper. It raised their spirits amazingly, and after their sparse meal, Rachel laid the map in front of them. It was a much-folded piece of yellow paper with a penciled drawing.

"Here we are near Bonn—across the bridge," she began. "I have to go into Belgium to Liège almost as the crow flies. My aunt Henrietta runs a cafe there called Le Café Meuse. It's a place where old men play dominoes and drink ale, and the young men come to make eyes at the girls." She laughed.

He was curious. "How do you know this? I thought you were only two years old when you left Belgium."

"I was, but my aunt wrote us such funny letters about the cafe. Poppo, the cook and headwaiter, insults the customers, and they love it. Sometimes the cafe is so busy that he lets the customers get their own coffee. Then when the espresso machine is empty, he runs around the room asking who drank all his coffee! My aunt says he usually picks out the most serious customer, then points at him and announces loudly, 'Here he is. This is the one who drank all my coffee!' "

They laughed together. "What will you do there?" Kurt asked.

"Work for my room and board. Aunt Henrietta always used to ask when I was going to spend the summer with her. She said I could wait on tables." Rachel lowered her head. "She never guessed she would have me for the rest of my life. But there's no use thinking about that now." She sat up straighter. "Liège. How far do you think it is from here?"

He studied the map. "Hmm. I'm going to say around a hundred kilometers. Maybe a bit more. Once across the bridge, you should see a sign pointing the way to Belgium; the border isn't very far."

"Good. We can make that. Do you think Fritz can walk well enough now?"

"Probably. But I . . . for me to cross that bridge is suicide."

"What else can you do?"

"I don't know. I can't stay here. I'm not safe in this uniform anywhere."

Rachel regarded him seriously for a long moment, head to one side, dark eyes surveying him, measuring him. Then she brushed the dark hair off her forehead and said, "I could steal some civilian clothes for you. There are bound to be some on the clotheslines in Erpel."

"But if I'm caught out of uniform, I could be shot as a spy!"

"Maybe they wouldn't guess you're a soldier. You do

look too young," she pointed out. "And if you're captured *in* uniform, you can probably guess what will happen to you."

"I don't need to guess. I know. They'll shoot me — my own army or the enemy." His blue eyes were worried now. He frowned. "All right. You can try for the clothes, but Fritz and I are going with you."

She looked horrified. "You can't! It's too dangerous!"

"What makes you think it's safe here?" he demanded. "The American soldiers will come back for the wine. I don't want to be trapped here!"

"I forgot about those soldiers." She was thoughtful for a minute. "Look, here's a plan. You and Fritz hide near that old tannery, and I'll go into the village. Agreed? If we get caught together, I'll say you're my brother and that we bought this uniform. Half the people in Erpel wear a piece of army clothing. I've seen them."

"But I don't look like —"

She folded her arms and glared at him. "Don't you dare say you don't look like a Jew! Just because I have dark hair and eyes doesn't mean all Jews look alike! The German people really think they're special, don't they!"

"Rachel, I was only going to say I don't look like you. I'm blond!"

"Hitler isn't blond! He's dark like me!" She stared fiercely at him, then relaxed. Finally she said, "Let's go now if we're going."

He nodded. They packed their few utensils in his backpack, took one last look around, and left the cave.

Fritz limped happily along with them, sniffing at

various animal holes in the woods. It was wet under the trees. They were half-soaked by the time they reached the tannery.

"You stay out of sight," she ordered. "Go around to the back of this building. It's empty, and I don't think anyone ever comes here."

He looked at her resentfully.

"You don't like having a girl do this when you can't, do you?"

He turned away without answering. He hated fighting with people.

"Especially a Jewish girl," she prodded.

"That's not fair!" he snapped. "I'd like to be able to help myself. Anyone would! And your being Jewish means absolutely nothing to me! You could be any girl from my school."

She put her hand on his arm. "I remember you," she joked. "You used to sit in the back and write down every word the teacher said!"

He relaxed and smiled at her. "And you sat in front and questioned every word out of the teacher's mouth!"

She smiled, and he noticed the dimples on either side of her mouth. "Wish me luck."

He gripped her shoulders hard. For a moment she thought he was going to hug her. Then he let go.

"Good luck!" he said tersely.

Rachel left Fritz and Kurt behind the tannery and walked on to the village. The air was so moisture-laden that she was afraid there wouldn't be any wash hanging outside. She headed toward the left side of the village, hoping she would not meet the woman who had talked with her on the last trip. As she went down a slight hill, she saw a line full of clothes hanging inside a wooden fence. If she hadn't been above it, the clothes would not have been visible. No one was in the yard or on the street as far as she could tell.

There must be a way in, she thought. *The sidewalk runs right by the fence.* She found the fence gate and opened it cautiously. The rusty hinges squeaked in protest. She winced but continued into the yard. *Still no one in sight. So far, so good.*

She examined the clothing. A woman's skirt, a man's long underwear. *Good. I'll take that.* She lifted it off the line. *Overalls! Perfect. He can wear the long underwear with the overalls over them. That's enough.* She reached for the faded overalls and paused. They were huge. *They'd go twice around Kurt's waist*, she thought. She couldn't see anything else which would help clothe him. As she jerked the overalls off the line, a fat man ran out the kitchen door. She recognized instantly that the overalls were a perfect fit for him.

"Here, you!" he yelled. "What are you doing with my clothes?" Puffing, he ran down the steps toward her.

In her alarm she dropped the clothes.

"Your — your things fell off the line," she said. "I was only trying to hang them up again." She tried to smile. "I know how my mother hates it when our washing gets all muddy on the ground!"

He reached for her wrist and held on tightly. "You're not from Erpel," he said, looking closely at her face. "You're stealing from me. I'm taking you straight to the constable."

Rachel was terrified. *The very thing I feared.* She panicked. *And he's too strong for me. How can I possibly get loose? Maybe if I can talk him away from all these houses . . .*

He forced her out the gate and began hustling her down the sidewalk toward the center of town.

Rachel tried to pull away from his tight grip, but it was useless.

"I'll go with you," she promised, "but first I'd better go back to that old tannery. The other things I . . . took are out there." If she could only lure him closer to Kurt and Fritz, maybe Kurt would see her predicament and think of something.

The man paused in the middle of the sidewalk and stared at her. "You've been here before!" he accused. "What did you steal?" He held her wrist tightly and Rachel winced.

"Nothing much," she stammered. "I was hungry! I was going to sell them in the next village. Just some clothes at . . . at . . ." Desperately she tried to remember the name of the woman who had stopped her the time before. What if this man took her to the constable and these people realized she was a Jew? Then what? "I took them from Frau Leibenstein's — stockings, and other clothes."

The man jerked her along a few steps, then stopped. "I did hear about somebody losing a pair of stockings off a line! Was that you? And what else?" he demanded. "You're going with me," he said roughly. "You can tell the constable all about your little thefts!"

"No," she pleaded. "Don't you want to see all the

things returned to their rightful owners? I'll show you where they're hidden. You can go with me. I won't be able to run away. You're far too strong for me."

The fat man scratched the stubble on his chin with his free hand. "All right," he said slowly, "but you needn't think I'm letting go of you, little lady!"

He jerked her around and began pulling her toward the edge of town. Although he maintained his grip, he was no longer squeezing her arm so tightly. She noticed thankfully that no one else appeared on the streets. When they reached the tannery, Rachel saw with relief that Fritz and Kurt were not visible.

Suddenly she yelled as loudly as she could, "Help, Fritz, help!"

Startled, the man lost his grip on her arm, then cringed as the huge dog bounded toward them, barking ferociously. Without a backward glance, the man scurried in the direction of his home. Rachel knelt by Fritz and embraced him.

"Stay, boy. It's okay," she whispered into his ear. The frantic dog obeyed but continued barking until the fat man had fled from sight.

"Come on, Fritz." The two ran to the back of the tannery. Kurt was nowhere to be seen, but Rachel thought she heard him running up the hill above her. She and Fritz followed as quickly as they could and soon caught up to him. Kurt turned his head once to glare back at her. She tried to look away from his accusing eyes.

When they reached the top of the hill, Fritz was ahead of them. He stopped and began to growl menacingly. The hair on the back of his neck bristled.

"What's he — " Rachel began before Kurt clapped his hand over her mouth.

"Wait, Fritz," he whispered urgently, and half dragged Rachel behind the same fallen tree where he and Fritz had hidden the day before. He took his hand off her mouth since the voices were clearly audible now. He pulled her to the ground and lay down beside her.

Soldiers! In the cave. This time we're finished, Rachel thought, heart pounding. *We were making so much noise coming up the hill!*

Kurt wondered if the dog had heard his command to wait. *Hopefully, the soldiers would think the dog had made all the noise in the woods,* he thought. *What will they think of the ashes from our fire?* Kurt pushed Rachel's head down and lowered his own. The two fugitives could see nothing but the log and the leaf-covered ground. They heard men's voices, evidently soldiers who were trying to coax Fritz to them with pleas and whistles. Neither Kurt nor Rachel understood what the Americans were saying.

After an eternity of nose-itching misery, the two heard a sharp command from below the cliff and the pounding of feet as soldiers left the cave and went down the hill.

For almost ten minutes, they were afraid to move. Fritz finally whined impatiently. Gradually Kurt lifted his head. He smiled to see the obedient Fritz waiting for the next command.

"Come, Fritz," he whispered, and the dog trotted over to them. They both stood and brushed off the leaves. Kurt signaled Rachel to wait for him but not too near the entrance. He listened for a few minutes, then went in.

After a space of time, he stood at the cave door and beckoned to her. Without a word, he took the blanket out of the pack and spread it for them to sit on. Fritz slumped in the corner licking his hurt paw. Kurt examined it momentarily.

"It's all right," he said in answer to Rachel's anxious eyes. "Only a little sore." Then he put his hands on his knees and took a deep breath.

Rachel pretended to be absorbed in the dog's slow licking as she gradually relaxed in the comparative safety of the cave.

"You tried to betray me," Kurt said flatly. "How could I have trusted you?"

"No!" Rachel said fiercely and sat up on her knees. "I told the man nothing about you. Believe me! When he caught me taking his dumb overalls off the line, I told him I had more stolen clothing at the tannery and would give it to him. Honestly, Kurt." She looked at him pleadingly. "I thought I could get away when Fritz came after him." She looked at Kurt belligerently. "It worked, too!"

"And if it hadn't? If he'd seen me? Rachel, that was a dangerous idea."

She shrugged helplessly. "I didn't know what else to do. I was already caught. I told you in the beginning that I was going to make it to Liège — no matter what I have to do to get there!"

Kurt sighed. "The important thing is we're safe now. I shouldn't have yelled at you. When I first saw the man with you, I thought — "

"I know. You thought I had betrayed you. For just a second," she confessed, "the thought may have crossed my mind. But we're in this together now, and we have to make it through safely—together." Her dark eyes stared solemnly into his blue ones. "Wars are between countries, not between two individuals like you and me. I do have one deep regret," she said, and the dimples quivered again beside her mouth.

"I should think you would. What you did was pretty risky."

"I do. I wanted to see you in that fat man's overalls and now I never will!" Then they laughed until they fell over on the blanket. When Fritz stood over them and started barking, they sat up.

"Kurt." She brushed her hair out of her eyes. "Come with me. Together we have a better chance of making it across the bridge. I'd feel safer with you along."

Kurt returned her now serious gaze. "All right," he said finally, "but if we get separated, you must keep going to Liège. Take Fritz and go on. Don't even look behind you if we're stopped. If they think you're with a German soldier, you'll be under suspicion, too. If I'm stopped, I'll follow you later. If I can," he added lamely.

Her dark eyes were apprehensive. "If the Americans stop you, they'll—"

"Nothing will happen," he said, and hoped it was true. "If we have a good plan, we'll get safely across the bridge. Will you give me your word to keep going if we're stopped? No funny games or anything like that?"

Rachel looked at him searchingly, then said, "I promise." She held out her right hand. They shook hands solemnly.

She smiled. "Now let's make our plan."

9

THE PLAN

The chill drove them to build another fire. Kurt hoped they would be gone before the American soldiers wondered about the ashes. It was possible the soldiers had seen the remains of the first fire and would come back to check. This time the twigs were wet, and the fire tended to smoke. Kurt kept the pile small and soon the flames settled down to a cheerful snapping and crackling.

"We'll have to cross the bridge in the dark. That's the only way I can hope to get to the other side in this uniform," he said. "We'll make use of their tape. How nice of them to string that wire for us!"

"How will we use it? It'll be as dark for us as it is for them."

"But we'll be on foot. We can *hold* the wire as we cross even if we can't see it. If it's as dark tonight as it has been the last two nights, they won't be able to see the white tape. Or us!" he concluded triumphantly.

"Tonight!" Rachel stared at him. "It's freezing out

there. Raining. Fritz isn't able to walk well enough. I don't see —"

Kurt looked stern. "It may rain for a month. And Fritz went up and down that big hill just fine. He's putting his sore paw on the ground a little now. How long do you think we can stay here without food?"

They both stared at the half loaf of bread that Rachel had unpacked from the knapsack and set on a nearby cask.

Kurt said, "That's it. That's all we have. And if I know soldiers, they'll be back as soon as it's daylight to get some of that wine. Now what do you say about leaving early tomorrow morning before daylight?"

"Tomorrow morning it is," Rachel said, her eyes wide and frightened. "Tomorrow morning."

"We need some way to stay close together," Kurt said. "It'll be very dark out there. I don't think you understand how dark it can be at night in a forest when it's raining. We won't even be able to see each other."

Rachel pulled her ruined stockings from her coat pockets. "What kind of chain can we make to keep the three of us from losing each other in the dark? Could you tie these together for a rope?"

Thrusting out his bottom lip, Kurt contemplated the torn cotton stockings. "Here. Give them to me." He held them together, stretching them out with the ends in each hand. He jerked sharply to see if the stockings would tolerate the strain.

"They were almost new when I left Berlin," Rachel said. "Ugly, but good strong material."

Kurt tied them together with a tight knot. "They'll do." Then he made a loop in one end of the tattered rope. He looked around for a moment, then tied the other end through the straps on the back of his knapsack.

"What are you doing?"

He fastened the pack over his shoulders and ordered, "Slip the loop over your left wrist."

"I see. What about Fritz?"

"I'll put my belt around his neck as a leash. He'll quite naturally want to walk ahead of us unless I tell him to heel. Crossing the bridge, we may make a change. We shouldn't be yoked together when we cross the bridge in case . . . in case . . ."

"In case you're stopped, you mean. You're scaring me."

He looked at her quietly, then said, "I'm afraid for both of us, but we can't stay here. I know this cave has come to mean security for you, but it isn't safe. The soldiers may return anytime. Either we'll starve to death, or the planes will come back again and again until they blow up the bridge and maybe part of this hill, too. As soon as the pilots figure out the Germans are no longer in control of the bridge, they'll be back, believe me!"

"I know. I'm ready. When's the best time to go?"

He removed the backpack. "We should eat once more. Then we'll have to wait until two hours before dawn. We have to go down the hill and cross the bridge in the dark, but you—we—won't know where to go once we're across unless it's almost daylight. We have to locate the road to Belgium early because of my uniform."

He looked at his watch. "It's almost seven o'clock. If we leave the cave by four, we should be across before dawn."

They gathered more wood for the fire, then settled down to wait. By now, Fritz was more active. He padded happily about the cave, occasionally scratching at the cave walls.

"He probably thinks he smells a rat," Kurt explained.

Rachel quickly drew her knees up and wrapped her arms around them. She frowned.

He laughed. "Don't worry. As hungry as Fritz is by now, the rat would never get past his nose!"

She relaxed her grip on her legs and grinned ruefully. "You're probably right. I'm hungry, too."

"You're always hungry, I think," he teased. "Let's prepare a sumptuous meal of bread—"

"And cheese."

"And a little touch of the grape." Kurt looked for the cup. "Where did the cup go?"

She searched through the pack. "Here. Wine will help keep us warm. It worries me a little that it's so cold and wet out there."

Kurt glanced out the cave entrance. Darkness had fallen, and a steady light drizzle whispered to the spring grass that struggled to emerge from the heavy blanket of leaves covering the ground.

"It'll soon be spring," he said wistfully. "Spring on a farm means new pigs. Lots of baby pigs. It means hauling manure to spread on our fields which began almost three kilometers from our house. We had the finest potatoes in Leipzig!" he said proudly.

Rachel groaned. "I wish I had one of your good pota-toes now!" She went over to the wall and searched through the stones next to it. Bringing back a large round rock about the size of her fist, she told him playfully, "I'm going to put this potato on a stick and roast it in the fire. Wait till you taste it!"

He reached for the rock with a serious expression. He took out the mess-kit knife and gravely scraped at the top of the rock.

"What are you doing?"

"Cutting a little piece off the top of the potato so it doesn't explode when it gets hot. Can't you cook?"

She shrieked with laughter. "I don't believe it! Kurt can joke! I didn't think it was possible!"

He allowed himself a tiny smile.

"What else did you do on your farm besides grow pota-toes?" she asked. "What's the worst chore you had to do? I've never lived in anything but apartments."

"Chase pigs."

"Chase pigs? Weren't they in a pen?"

"Pigs root under fences. They keep digging until they get out or maybe knock down a board or two. Then they run wild, and someone has to chase them. I remember one night"—he chuckled—"the pigs were out and some of our cows got out of the barn. They were all running around the outside of our house in the middle of the night. Katzi thought we were surrounded by Bolsheviks—what an imagination! She cried until Pa and I went out and rounded them up. It took us all night to get them back in and the pig fence temporarily mended."

Rachel giggled.

"It wasn't funny to me," he insisted. "I had to fix fences all the rest of that week!" He looked at her seriously for a moment, then said hesitantly. "You accused me once of not knowing anything about the Jews. I guess you're right. What was it like for you?"

She raised her eyebrows. "The war was going long before you knew it was! In 1938, all my friends were moved to Jewish schools, not as good as your schools were."

"Your friends? What about you?"

"No one knew we were Jewish. We had come from Belgium where my aunt and grandmother live, and . . . no one knew. We didn't attend synagogue. As soon as my parents saw the way things were going for our people, they wouldn't even let us discuss our heritage."

"But you weren't safe anyway."

"No," she said sadly. "And we were always afraid. We tried to observe the Sabbath, but it was always very secret."

He looked puzzled. "How do you observe the Sabbath if you can't go to church — synagogue, I mean?"

She looked around the cave at the loaf of bread and casks of wine. "It would begin with special wine and bread," she said. "The Sabbath really starts for us on Friday evening, but before dark. My mother would light the candles on the table, at least two. She didn't look at the candles, though."

"Why?" he asked.

"That comes later. First she would say the blessing. Then my father would say another blessing, and we would all drink wine from a kiddush cup. The loaves of hallah bread would be covered with a cloth until we were ready for them. There is a special blessing over the hallah.''

He nodded. "Like communion, kind of."

She was pleased at his understanding. "Yes! And the food was really special for that meal." She looked down sadly. "We didn't dare do even that during the last year. Kyle was so young; my parents were afraid he would talk about it and we would be caught. Also, we never knew when a knock would come at the door and it would all be over for us."

"At your grandmother's," Kurt said hopefully, "you won't have to be afraid to observe your religion."

He stood up and twisted the metal handle of the wine tap hard. Wine flowed easily into the cup. He set the cup on the ground in front of him. Rachel cut the bread ceremoniously with little flourishes of the mess-kit knife, smiling at Kurt. She sliced the remaining chunk of cheese into three parts. Fritz stopped scratching the wall and slumped into his corner, sniffing at the cheese odor.

"Here, boy." Breaking tiny bits off the last slice of cheese, Kurt fed the dog. "He loves this."

She nodded.

As she reached for a piece of bread, Kurt said, "Wait! I think we should do something special on our last night here. I feel the need of — of something. What day of the week is it?"

Her wide eyes stared at him. "I don't know."

"Then I say it is the Sabbath. We shall celebrate your holy day together."

"But we have no candles — no cloth for the bread — nothing!"

She could tell how disappointed he was. He looked around the cave and turned to her beseechingly.

"Rachel, we are in a cave in the middle of a war! And tomorrow we may be . . . captured, or . . . or worse."

Rachel's eyes began to sparkle. "We will be inventive. We'll pretend it's Friday night!"

Kurt searched through the pile of kindling and bigger pieces of wood for the fire. He finally pulled out a gnarled hunk which had two large knotholes. He laid it on the blanket directly in front of their crossed legs.

Guessing what he had in mind, Rachel picked up several small pieces of kindling, trying each in the knotholes. Finally she found two that fit. She removed them and laid them down carefully. She placed the last pieces of their bread on the blanket. They looked around the cave for a cover. There was nothing.

Kurt folded a corner of the blanket over the bread, and Rachel smiled at him. She jumped up and took her black scarf from her coat pocket, draping it over her head.

"The cup is full of wine," she said. "It is our kiddush cup. Now if I can only remember the words — "

"They will come to you," he comforted, "like all prayers you have learned. Think about your mother and listen to her voice."

At last everything was ready. Rachel took the two small pieces of wood, lit each in turn from the fire, and poked it into the small log. Then she covered her eyes with her fingers. After several false starts, she began to sing in a low, sweet voice.

"Baruch-ata-Adonai, Eloheynu melech haolam, asher kid'shanu b'mitzvosav, v'tzeevanu l'hadleek ner shel Shabbes." Knowing his unfamiliarity with the Hebrew, she began again in German. "Blessed is the Lord, Ruler of the Universe, who has commanded us to kindle the lights on the Sabbath."

Kurt looked at her in wonder. There was a mystical light in her face as she lowered her hands, and flames from the burning sticks reflected in her dark eyes.

"Is it all right if I say 'Amen'?" he whispered. She nodded. "Amen."

Kurt handed her the cup politely with a small bow. She held up the wine and said the "kiddush" blessing softly. She sipped the wine, then returned the cup. She broke off a little piece of the bread, handed Kurt half, and said the blessing as if the bread were hallah. They ate the bread and cheese slowly, knowing it was their last meal together in the cave.

Rachel studied him. *What a strange mixture he was! He understood nothing of his country's politics and knew little about the war.* His simple request to share a Sabbath meal had touched her.

Soon the cheese was gone, and Rachel put the rest of the bread into the knapsack.

"Let's see," Rachel said. "I'll wait on tables in Le Café Meuse and finish my schooling. What will you do?"

He tried to rally to her dreams of a future that he doubted would materialize for either of them. "Kurt will be . . . will be . . . let's see." He looked at Fritz. "A veterinarian. That's it, a veterinarian!"

She put her hands on her hips, pursed her lips, then nodded. "That's a very good idea! You would make a fine animal doctor. And I, I will be your assistant!"

They forced smiles at each other over the cup of wine while the cold rain fell steadily outside. An impenetrable darkness closed in over the forest and the bridge.

10

DOWN THE HILL

*R*achel finally fell asleep soundly, but Kurt slept in a world of half-dreams, interrupted by involuntary starts. He feared he wouldn't wake up in time. During his brief, troubled encounters with sleep, his dreams were strange, distorted wanderings. In most of them he found himself hopelessly lost, staggering through overgrown meadows or blundering across an endless bridge that had no sides. He woke up sweating.

He held up his watch to the dying flames. *Not yet.* He wondered how the Americans did away with their prisoners. His captains had stressed the dangers of being captured and the horrors of surrender.

"The Allies pursue a 'scorched earth' policy," Captain Bratge had told the Fifth Panzer Division Demolition Company. "Our Führer has told us this. They will burn everything to the ground and kill all Germans — civilians or otherwise — as they march through Germany. That is why we must stop them. There will be nothing left of our homeland if we fail."

Kurt lay back restlessly. *Could we swim the river?* He

rejected the idea instantly. The river was over three hundred and fifty meters wide at this point, its temperature close to freezing, and the current ran at a speed of two meters per second.

Even if Rachel can swim, we would be swept downstream to certain death by drowning. If no one shot us first!

He decided not to sleep, but awoke with a jerk a few hours later. The fire was reduced to glowing coals. He had to strike a match to see his watch. *Almost time.*

Rachel. He watched her sleep for a few moments. She looked so peaceful, he dreaded awakening her to reality.

In the dim light from his match, her black hair streamed out over the knapsack, which she used as a pillow. Once again her hands were clenched even in sleep. *What a brave fighter she is*, he thought. *She deserves to get through to safety. Life has to hold more for her than this.* He looked around. *If we're lucky, we'll never see this cave again.* He felt as if he should write their names on the casks or scratch them on the walls, but he had nothing to write with. He threw a handful of dried leaves onto the burning coals and when they flamed, he picked up the dipper and laboriously scratched their initials into the side of a cask with the long handle of the dipper.

K. M.
&
R. G.
1945

It was time. "Rachel. Rachel." She looked up at him blankly as if wondering where she was.

"I'm ready," she said sleepily.

He showed her what he had carved. She nodded as if in approval but said nothing. He realized she was too worried about crossing the bridge to think of anything else.

They searched the cave for their meager supplies, re-packed the knapsack, and checked the connecting "rope." Rachel draped the black scarf over her head and tied it under her chin. She pulled on her gloves and grasped the end of the rope, slipping the loop over her left wrist.

"Ready," she repeated.

Kurt placed his belt again around Fritz's neck. He knelt by the big dog and embraced him. "Good boy, Fritz. Keep quiet, now." The dog licked Kurt's ear affectionately.

"Let's go," the boy said gruffly.

They left the cave and plunged immediately into the most complete darkness Rachel had ever experienced. She caught her breath in alarm. Kurt turned around.

"I have the direction in mind. We'll head for the motor noise from the trucks crossing the bridge. If you want to stop me for some reason and are afraid to call out, make two quick tugs on the rope. Try it."

Obediently she jerked the rope twice.

"That's it. Let's go."

Fritz was the only one who seemed happy to be out in the damp, cold night. He trotted alongside Kurt, who walked deliberately with his left arm raised in front of him to ward off sudden contact with a tree. Countless branches struck his outstretched arm. As he forced his way down the hill and through the woods, he prayed Rachel was short enough to escape being slapped in the face by the rebounding branches.

At one point he slipped on the pebbled hillside and fell, sliding forward on his seat. Caught by surprise, Rachel followed him — also in a sitting position — and they wound up in a tangled heap in a wet bush. Fritz jumped happily on top of them. Rachel giggled, and they got painfully to their feet.

"You're going too fast," Rachel spoke into his ear. "We'll break our necks at this rate. Slow down!"

Kurt nodded, then realized she couldn't see him. He put his mouth up to her ear. "I'll take it slower. Are you all right?"

"Yes."

They groped their way down the hill, getting wetter and colder by the moment. Water dripped down their necks from the damp overhanging branches. As the heavy vehicles rumbled in their direction, the whine of changing gears became louder. Kurt heard the heavy swirling waters of the river. When he thought they were close enough, he stopped and turned around. Still hanging on to Fritz's leash, he caught Rachel by the shoulders. He put his head next to hers.

"We're going to make a shift now. We're almost at the bridge. I think you can get us to the other side. I'm going to strap the pack on your back. You lead Fritz by the leash, and I'll hold the backpack by its strap. The rope puts us too far apart for the actual crossing."

His face was close to her cold, wet cheek in the dark. "Hold on to the wire with your right hand when you find it. That wire separates us from the trucks. On your left will be the bridge barricade. It's a wooden wall about a meter in height. Guide Fritz with your left hand. If he gets too far ahead, a tug on the belt will tell him."

He could feel her nodding in agreement. He held her tightly for a moment and then said, "You promised, remember? You and Fritz go on if we're stopped." He felt her head shake slightly in the negative. "You promised."

Then in the darkness, in the wet, miserable night, Kurt felt her warm lips on his cheek. Her face was wet with rain. *Tears?* He couldn't be sure. She turned and he helped her strap the pack onto her back. He removed the stocking rope and threw it away. He pushed the wet belt leash into her hand and grasped the pack strap.

"Go. Get us to the left side of the bridge. Remember the wooden wall on your left, the wire on your right. There will be a slight step down to the roadbed. We mustn't fall over the wire into the pathway of those trucks."

They stumbled forward into the growing noise of the heavy vehicles traveling without lights. The grinding of engines filled their ears. Suddenly Kurt's knee bumped against planks. He felt the wood carefully. They were at the barricade. *The bridge!* Rachel half turned as if to tell him, but he pushed her forward. They were on the bridge. Half a kilometer of stark terror lay before them.

11

CROSSING THE RHINE

*R*achel moved cautiously ahead. She touched the wooden wall with her left knee whenever she became disoriented. She held the leash in her left hand, but Fritz showed no signs of barging ahead. Instead he stepped gingerly on the planks, which occasionally had wide cracks between them.

The engines whined, roared, and sputtered alternately as different-sized vehicles passed them on the right. They could have leaned over and touched the fenders. The three inched their way along the narrow pathway between the bridge railing and the wire.

Rachel was grateful for the wire. *None of the drivers can possibly see the wire, even wrapped in white tape,* she thought, *but it's saving our lives.* She and Kurt held it in their right hands as if it were an umbilical cord.

They groped blindly on their way through this hell of rain and darkness. They stumbled ahead, praying with every step that the next one would not bring them up against a khaki-clad American. On and on they wavered through the unrelenting blackness. The uncaring waters of the river swept along under their feet more than seventy meters down. Machines groaned past the three, sometimes butting the tailgates in front of them in the dark night. No driver could see the vehicle in front of his. He could only hope he followed at a good interval. He was saved from going too far on one side by a low curb and by a wooden barricade on the other.

Suddenly the driver of the rumbling vehicle beside them leaned out the window to call to the truck behind him. Rachel was startled and stopped.

"Hey, you b——! You're climbin' my frame," the driver in front yelled. Bewildered by the phrases in English, which neither of them understood, they cowered against the wooden barricade until the truck lumbered on.

Rachel led them forward. *If there wasn't so much noise from the trucks and jeeps,* Kurt thought, *Fritz's toenails would click on the bridge planking. Good old Fritz! Not a sound from him yet.*

A faint change, discernible perhaps only to a straining ear, informed Kurt they had passed the middle of the bridge and were approaching the open side, the west bank. This bank had no cliffs behind it, only the open road. They successfully passed the first set of watchtowers without detection. Without warning, Fritz stopped. Kurt bumped into Rachel who was standing still. She reached back and gripped Kurt's right hand. He thought she might be laughing because he could feel her body shake. Then Kurt realized Fritz was urinating against the wooden side of the bridge. *Trust her to think that's funny!* They started again.

The rain continued, a light, cold drizzle that seemed to penetrate to their skin. As the tone changed to one of open rather than closed terrain, Kurt's hopes began to rise. They were gaining on the west bank, and no one had stopped them yet. His worries had been foolish. *We're going to make it!*

On and on they stumbled. Even the Rhine sounded different here without a cliff to absorb the sound of running water. The walk seemed endless. Rain fell on their soggy shoulders. Kurt stopped trying to brush away the rivulets of water dripping down his face. Still they walked.

Fritz bumped Rachel's leg as if in warning. Then she sensed rather than saw the watchtower ahead, much as a blind person becomes aware of objects. She stretched her right hand out in front of herself and in a few more steps ran into the stone tower. Kurt bumped into her, then backed off.

She inched slowly around the tower, which was round and almost blocked the walkway. Scraping their palms against the rough tower stones, they felt their way.

As they rounded the last few feet, the tower door opened in Kurt's face. He dropped his hold on the pack strap and sensed Rachel moving away from him. Carrying a rifle, the guard walked out casually and flipped a glowing cigarette butt into the black river below. Faint light from within the tower shone for a moment on the bulky vehicles grinding down the bridgeway. As the guard turned to go back inside, he walked straight into Kurt's arms.

"What the hell?" The guard raised his rifle and in the

dim light from the open door, Kurt saw the startled sergeant inside snatch his gun from behind a desk and run to the door.

As it swung shut, Kurt had a flashing glimpse of Rachel's straight back, her arm extended to hold Fritz's leash. She did not turn or betray by a glance that she knew of anything happening behind her although she must have felt him release his hold on the pack.

The guard barked an order in English. Puzzled, Kurt stood still. The sergeant charged from the tower door.

"Hände hoch!" he shouted, and Kurt raised his hands, linking them over his head as he had been told to do if captured. The dismal rain continued to fall as the sergeant herded his prisoner into the watchtower.

Outside the tower, Rachel walked steadily along the bridge walkway, her left hand gripping the leash, her right hand holding a taped wire. Tears mixed with rain streamed down her face. Dawn began to lift the darkness as she reached the west bank.

TO BELGIUM, the road sign read. Belgium — passage to freedom. Or despair.

12

KILLER

*W*hen the tower door had opened, Rachel's heart had jumped. She had felt the release of Kurt's grip on the backpack, but she had kept going straight ahead. Fritz had stopped. She jerked the leash and he started again, growling under his breath. She marched — it seemed more like a thousand meters than twenty — to the end of the bridge boardwalk.

She felt the cold emptiness of the night as she had not felt it before. When the planks ceased rattling under her feet, she paused uncertainly. Fritz panted beside her, although he turned anxiously several times to look back at the bridge. Once he pulled sharply against the leash as if to return to the tower.

"Here! Come back, Fritz!" she whispered harshly. "He's gone. We have to go ahead without him."

She walked to the nearest road, then on impulse turned to her left. She went a few meters and stopped. She turned and considered the bridge behind her.

A cold, gray dawn chewed away at the night's darkness. Vehicles ground across the giant causeway. The waters of the Rhine, the last real obstacle to the Allies, eddied and swirled beneath the Remagen Bridge, Carrying debris from the south of this great crumbling country to the north.

The water thundered on under the bridge, which was now weakened from the German bomb assault and threatening to collapse. Unseen damage to the bottom girders drained the strength of the bridge, this last link over the Rhine that the Americans had not expected to find standing.

As the sky cleared, Rachel's spirits darkened. She was facing exactly what she had feared: being alone again. *Not alone completely.* Fritz looked up at her with a "what now?" expression and wagged his tail. With a good strong shaking, he could rid himself of most of his moisture, but Rachel was hopelessly soaked.

STOLBERG 50 KM, the sign read. The road to Bonn led north. She knew she couldn't go that way. Stolberg was supposed to be about fifty kilometers from Liège. That would be her direction.

The sun came up, but it was a delusion. It warmed nothing. Not the barren, stripped earth nor the shivering girl and her companion. She sat, feeling empty as a gourd, wondering where she was going and why she was going there. As a small truck stopped beside her with three bearded civilians in the front seat, she stared at them as if they were intruders from outer space.

"Would you like a ride somewhere?" one of the men asked. He leered at her from the window.

"What?" Rachel stammered.

"Where do you want to go, Liebchen?" The question came again with much elbow poking in the truck cab.

"Liège," she said slowly. "Liège, I guess."

"Then come on, Schatzi, jump in the back," the caller invited. His accent was Belgian, the girl decided.

Rachel looked back at the bridge. There was no sign anything had happened on the bridge other than a river flowing under it or troops passing over it. She saw no prisoners and no prison compound. It would be useless to wait here for Kurt.

"Danke schoen," she said mechanically and climbed into the truck bed. Fritz leaped in beside her. The vehicle began to move as the three men alternately ogled her through the back window or laughed as the old truck chugged along. She leaned against the cab and hugged Fritz to her. A cold wind bit her wet skin. She looked back at the river for as long as she could see it.

The river was a dark ribbon of destiny, dividing a country whose fields and hills were even now being invaded. It might be decades before the scars and burn marks were obliterated from its ancient countryside. Soon Rachel could no longer see the river or the bridge.

The truck rattled and bumped along the shell-torn road. Rachel tried not to notice the constant glances of the three men. She suspected they were passing a bottle to each other. Her body felt like a bag of bruised bones, and the jolting of the truck made her ill. The vehicle had gone about ten kilometers when it turned off the main road onto a smaller one and bumped to a stop. She had no idea if this was still the route she wanted to be on.

After what seemed to be an argument, all three men got out and walked around to the back of the truck, looking expectantly at her and grinning. The man who had been sitting in the middle jumped into the truck bed. Beside her, Fritz tensed under her overlapping arm.

The man wore baggy black pants and a stained jacket with a red handkerchief tied around his neck. As he came closer, Rachel smelled wine and garlic and observed his black decayed teeth. He gave her a toothy smile.

Without warning, thirty-five kilos of dog dynamite slammed into the man. The two crashed to the ground behind the truck. Ominous growls and high-pitched, excited barks burst from Fritz as he stood over the surprised prone figure. The other two men backed off in terror and extended no helping hand to their frightened companion. The man on the ground looked up at the savagely angry dog standing above him.

Rachel jumped from the back of the truck. She picked up the end of Fritz's leash. Then she elaborately removed the belt and rolled it up in her hands. She glared at the three men who cowered visibly.

"My dog has been trained to kill. You'd better not make any sudden moves." She looked at Fritz who stood waiting for her command. "Come on, Killer, *we* will go back to the road. And you" — she pointed scornfully at the man who sprawled in front of her — "get into the truck and take your friends with you!"

The girl clucked a forward summons to Fritz, who was reluctant to move. "Heel!" she ordered, and he bounded to her side keeping a watchful eye on the men. Rachel and Fritz walked back to where the small country road joined the main road. She hoped it was the one to Stolberg. She shook in a chill such as she had never known, but she held her back stiffly as she walked away.

Behind her, the three men scrambled into the truck and with a great shifting of gears, barged ahead on the side road.

When the truck was out of sight, she knelt, crying, and hugged the big dog. He licked her tears and barked excitedly. He wagged his tail furiously. He looked at her as if he wondered why she was crying. Finally she blew her nose on Kurt's dirty handkerchief. Recognizing it brought a few more tears.

It's not going to be easy to get to Liège, but that's where we're going. With a stubborn set to her chin, she moved down the main road.

13

THE FARM

*R*achel and Fritz stood for a long time just beyond the intersection of the two roads. She wanted to make it clear to anyone passing which direction she was going — to Liège, hopefully, via the Stolberg road. No one came so she sat down under a towering oak tree and unpacked the bread from the knapsack. She looked at the bread mournfully. Then with a sigh she fed the dog a few morsels of bread and ate the rest.

"I'm really sick of eating just plain bread," she told the dog. "You probably are, too." A tail wag was her only answer. They sat for hours. If she had been positive that this was the road to Stolberg, she would have tried walking a few kilometers on it. She knew that with the front line of battle so close, few vehicles other than military would be on the road except for local ones like the truck. She shivered in her wet clothing. The day was not warm enough to dry it.

Quite late in the afternoon, a vehicle approached. As it lumbered to the crossroad, she saw it was an old farmer driving a wagon with two enormous horses pulling it.

Rachel ran toward the wagon waving her arms. The old man looked at her and spoke to halt the horses.

"Whoa, Toby, whoa Geri," he called. He pulled back on the reins and when the wagon stopped rolling, laid the reins over his ample lap.

"What is it, Fraülein?"

"Are you going in the direction of Stolberg — toward Liège?"

The old farmer cupped his ear. "To where?" he shouted.

"To Stolberg! Is that where this road goes?"

"Yes, that's where it goes, but I'm going only a little way down the road. Do you want a lift?"

"Please," Rachel entreated.

"Hop up on this seat," the farmer suggested. "Your dog can sit by our feet. It's only a two-seated wagon. I'm afraid the wagon is very dirty. I've been hauling manure to my fields."

They scrambled onto the front seat of the wagon, which Rachel thought smelled cleaner than the truck had. She smiled at the old farmer as he chirped to his horses.

The man stole little glances at the girl as they rode. He was obviously curious about her presence on the road but too polite to question it.

"Old Toby and Geri been with me twenty years," he told the girl with pride. "They can haul an army tank out of the ditch if need be. They're Percherons." The horses slogged on through the mud. As they neared a narrow trail which left the main road, he peeked at the exhausted girl.

"M'wife's waiting supper. Care to stop with us for a bit of food?"

There was a long silence. Rachel leaned over the dog. At last she said, "Fritz is very hungry. Thank you."

The wagon turned down a small roadway. Once around the corner, they drew up in front of an old brick U-shaped building. The left arc of the semicircle was evidently a house. The farmer shuffled up the steps. At the right stood a barn with a hayloft. Connecting the house and the barn was a toolshed. Several shovels leaned against its door. The courtyard in the center had a pit half-filled with manure from the barn.

Within a few minutes a plump woman emerged, wiped her hands on a flour-sack apron, and peered nearsightedly at the forlorn girl. Rachel shivered and wondered if she would be safe here.

"Come on in, miss," the woman called. "If you like potato soup, we have plenty."

By this time Rachel was so tired she felt she could topple from the wagon into a hedge and never notice. She dismounted from the wagon. Fritz leaped down. He nosed joyously ahead, barking at the chickens that wandered up to the wagon.

"No, Fritz," Rachel said sharply. The dog lay down near the steps, head on his paws, watchful eyes on the girl. "Stay!" she commanded, and followed the woman into the house.

"Give me that pack and your wet coat," the housewife ordered. "I will hang the coat near the stove so it will dry." She bustled around the kitchen hanging up the coat and setting a place for the girl at the table.

"Sit there. Here is a bowl of hot soup. Meat we do not have now. You swallow this down, and I will go feed your nice dog."

So many delightful food aromas filled the small kitchen that Rachel's stomach shook. The woman plopped a large bowl of soup down on the oilcloth-covered table. She added bread, a little dish of home-made butter, and a big glass of milk.

Dazed, Rachel stared around the kitchen. It was another world—so civilized that the girl was unable to handle the sudden change in life-styles. The floor was covered with linoleum so faded that it was gray, but scrubbed clean and shiny. Decorative plates, framed mottoes, calendar pictures, and crocheted dolls hung on the walls. The soup smelled wonderful. After the first burning sip, she spooned the soup slowly into her mouth. The glass of milk was so creamy she could not believe it was merely milk. Steam rose from her wet coat. *Not a pleasant smell,* she thought, *but I'll need a dry coat when I leave.*

The farmer's wife returned. She dusted her hands on her apron. "Your dog is starving. Did you know that?"

Rachel nodded. The woman noticed the empty soup bowl and filled it again, darting quick glances at Rachel's wet clothes and scratched face. When the girl pushed away the empty bowl and leaned her chin on her hand with one tired elbow on the table, the woman studied her curiously. She folded her arms over her apron and plump little stomach.

"You do not care for any bread and butter?"

Rachel shook her head slowly. Explanations were beyond her. In spite of herself, her eyes wanted to close.

"My name is Hilda, and my husband is Wilhelm. I do not know from where you came, but I can tell a wet, worn-out child when I see one. You need a good sleep, but not in a bed of mine without a bath. Come now." And seeing the girl's inquiring look, she added, "Your dog is fine. Wilhelm took him to the barn. Come."

Rachel was surprised. "Fritz went with him?"

"Papa has a way with animals," she said, switching her head proudly. "Tonight your Fritz will sleep in a nice, warm barn with the cows and horses."

Hilda snatched a bucket of boiling water from the top of the kitchen stove. "This way." She beckoned with her free hand. She led the way upstairs into a large, chilly bathroom. She set the steaming bucket down next to the claw-footed tub.

"Here," she said. "Your wet clothes you will put outside the door. Pour the hot water into the tub and let in the cold water. The soap I made. It is not the best, but it is all we have now. I will put a warm nightgown on the back of the door and I will make ready a bed."

Rachel was beyond speech. After Hilda marched out, Rachel undressed and placed her filthy, wet clothes outside the bathroom door. Dreamily, she poured the bucket of hot water into the tub, let in some cold water, and got in with a heartfelt sigh. She slipped down into the tub until her hair was under the water. She lingered there until she realized the water would cool off rapidly in the cold room.

Although she tried to get suds into her dirty hair from the homemade soap, she could not. She lay down again and rinsed her hair, then sat up and smoothed back the sleek dripping strands. She soaped and rinsed her entire body, lying there until her fingers puckered in the water. Then she reluctantly stood up and got out of the tub.

She rubbed her wet head with a towel, then leaned over and swept her long hair under it, wrapping the towel around her head turban-fashion. She reached for another towel to dry herself. The towels were clean but thin and a kind of noncolor as if they had been washed and bleached so many times that the original hue had been lost.

Hesitantly she opened the bathroom door. Her clothes were gone. A long flannel nightgown swung from the hook on the other side, also a blue plaid bathrobe with a cord belt. She lifted them off the hook and brought them into the bathroom. Dressed, she stared at herself in the small fogged mirror, first rubbing a clear oval in the middle.

It was a reflection she hardly recognized. The mirror image showed enormous black eyes, a rosy face with many scratches, and a dull blue bruise over the left temple. She supposed it was from going down the hill in the dark and getting hit in the face with a tree branch. The mouth was wide and full, tremulous now. She was so exhausted.

She touched her face. She was clean and warm and full of good food. *Where was Kurt?* She stared at the stranger in the mirror, remembering.

She cleaned the tub with hands and arms so tired that

they did not seem to be part of her body. She picked up the bucket and carried it back down to the kitchen. The two old people were finishing the potato soup. The old man waved her to a rocking chair by the stove.

"Dry your hair, child. Your dog is comfortable in the barn with Toby and Geri and the cows."

Rachel sat down in the chair. The heat, the warm food, and the bath had taken their toll. She didn't believe she was capable of speech. She removed the towel and leaned her seal-like head against the high back of the chair.

"Thank you," she managed weakly. She noticed her clothes soaking in a small tub on top of the wood stove, but she was too tired to question or protest. She rocked slowly in the chair as her hair dried in the warm kitchen. When Hilda handed her an old-fashioned round hair-brush, she accepted it without a word. She dragged it through her long hair over and over again until her hair lay like a black silken mantle over her shoulders.

"Come, Liebchen," the old lady said briskly.

What a different sound it has in her mouth, Rachel thought, remembering the man in the truck. She followed Hilda up the stairs again and into a bedroom. Hilda stuffed a heated brick wrapped in cloths down into the old-fashioned brass bed that almost filled the bedroom. The headboard was taller than Rachel and the foot half as high. The brass bars that formed the bed ends were clumsily rounded and dented in many places, although they shone from housewifely attention.

"Give me the robe now and under the covers you go," Hilda directed. She gave Rachel a little nudge toward the bed. Rachel took off the robe and handed it to Hilda who laid it across the bottom of the bed.

"Get in. What's your name, child?"

"Rachel," the girl said, dull-eyed and exhausted. "Rachel Gildemeister." She crawled into the bed and put her clean feet on the warm stone. She did not see Hilda pull up the covers nor sense the light going out.

14

THE ROAD TO LIÈGE

*R*achel awoke to find sunlight streaming into the single window near her head. It took her a few seconds to remember where she was.

Linoleum picturing blue feathery plumes covered the floor. A dark oak dresser squatted in the right-hand corner. Covering its top was a clean embroidered scarf. It reminded her of one she had started for her mother and never finished. A large hand mirror lay upside down on the scarf. Instead of a door, a blue-flowered curtain hung in front of a closet on the left. The room smelled musty, as if it had been closed for some time.

She got out of bed and put on the robe. She wondered where her clothes were and hoped they were dry. She made the bed and descended the steps to the kitchen. Hilda was poking at the fire in the kitchen stove. She slammed the round stove lid on, then looked up.

"Well, well. Rachel, is it? Sit down, Rachel, and see what our good hens have left for you!" She held up two enormous brown eggs. "That is all the Americans took when they passed by here. A few chickens and some eggs.

Our neighbors were afraid they would burn all our houses when they came, but they didn't." She turned back to the stove to crack the eggs into a pan.

Rachel sat down at the table. Her clothes were draped on hangers precariously hooked over the edge of a shelf. Everything looked wrinkled but dry.

"Thank you for washing my clothes," the girl said. "I've been wearing them quite a while."

"I was happy to do it." Hilda did not turn around from the stove. "You are welcome to look through the parlor next to this room, although it is not heated. Beyond that is the toolshed and then the barn. You can see that after breakfast. Go on, look!"

Rachel went through a swinging door into the parlor. A shelf in front of several windows held African violets, ivies, and other green plants. An old, brown radio with a curved top sat among the plants. This floor was also covered with linoleum. Big cabbage roses with large leaves formed the pattern. Small braided rugs lay in front of the brown mohair couch and also by the largest chair, a tall wooden armchair with needlepoint-covered seat and back.

She regarded the small rugs, remembering the many hours she had spent sewing rags for her mother to braid into rugs. *Was someone else walking on them now?* She couldn't bear the thought and pushed it away.

On the wall the pendulum of an old clock swept gently back and forth. Numerous objects stood on top of a tall narrow dresser: a white hobnailed vase held pink artificial flowers, shriveled orange berries protruded from a brown clay pot, a tiny can offered pencils and pens, a gold oval picture framed a smiling woman holding a baby dressed in a long baptismal gown. Several pictures of young men in German uniforms sat on the dresser. *I am in the home of my enemy,* Rachel thought sadly. *What has this war done to people?* Hilda called her name.

"I have to leave right after breakfast," Rachel told her as she ate the eggs. The plump woman began shaking her head. "Yes, I do. My aunt is — is expecting me in Liège." Rachel thought for a moment of how wonderful it would be to stay, allow someone to take care of her for a change. But more than anything else, she needed to know she still had her aunt and her grandmother. She must get to Liège.

Hilda accepted this without further argument but insisted on packing a lunch. "I am putting in some sandwiches made with my good apple butter," she said, "from our own apples. You will like it. My boys loved it."

After Rachel dressed, Hilda said, "Go out to the barn to see Papa's cows. He's very proud of his Holsteins."

Rachel felt timid walking to the barn. Being on a farm was a new experience for her. She pushed open the barn door and stood inside. Wilhelm was milking. He nodded happily to Rachel, squirting milk into the pail with both hands.

Fritz escaped through the open barn door and padded happily around the farmyard, sniffing along with his nose almost on the ground.

A deep layer of straw covered the barn floor, and Rachel enjoyed scuffing through it to the old man. At first she was afraid to touch the cows, but finally she patted one experimentally. The short bristly hairs delighted her. The cow's warm, muscular shoulder shrugged under her hand. Where the skin had been scratched, there were scabs here and there on the creature's body.

"Here," Wilhelm called to her. "Come try your hand at milking. It is easy. Squeeze and pull down at the same time," he directed, but even though Rachel squeezed as hard as she could, she was unable to extract a single drop of milk. The old cow turned her head and even with a mouthful of hay managed to convey her disapproval. Wilhelm took over and showed off by squirting milk directly into the face of a waiting gray cat. Rachel laughed to see the cat frantically licking its whiskers.

She helped Wilhelm carry the pails of milk to the house. In the warm kitchen she tried to tell the two old people how she felt about their kindness. She sensed their curiosity about her, but it would probably be better if they didn't know she was Jewish. The less they knew, the better. Until she reached her aunt's cafe, she dared not let down her guard.

"I want to say thank you in some way." She felt in the pocket of her coat. "Here are a few cigarettes. They were given to me by—by a German soldier, and I don't smoke." She raised her eyebrows at Wilhelm, who nodded his gray head.

"It has been a long time since I have had any cigarettes, and I will enjoy them," the old man said graciously.

"May you reach Liège in safety," Hilda said, handing Rachel a small piece of paper. "We have written our address for you. Let us know that you are safe, Liebchen.

"I will," Rachel promised.

Once again Rachel and Fritz climbed into the creaking old wagon, and with many waves and smiles between them, left Hilda standing on the back steps. Old Wilhelm insisted on staying with Rachel until a neighbor and his wife came along in an old car with two small tow-headed children bobbing up and down in the backseat like rubber balls. After a brief visit between the driver and Wilhelm, the children made room for the girl and her dog.

The children caressed Fritz all the way to Stolberg, but he endured it good-naturedly. The driver insisted on taking Rachel through the town so that she could find a ride to Liège more easily.

On every side Rachel saw piles of rubble where shells or bombs had destroyed shops and houses. Shell holes peppered the street itself, and the ancient car bumped tortuously through them. On top of one store front, a huge banner proclaimed, WELCOME AMERICANS.

The storekeeper's not taking any chances, Rachel decided. *The last sign he put up probably read*, HEIL HITLER!

For the first time it occurred to her that perhaps Le Café Meuse no longer existed. *Was it a heap of rubble as these shops were?* And her aunt . . . her grandmother? If they were gone, what would she do?

At the town's outer edge where the road sign stated, LIÈGE 60 KM, the car stopped. Fritz leaped out and sat patiently by Rachel as she waited for a ride.

After the car left, Rachel sagged dejectedly against the signpost, feeling depressed at the thought of the cafe being only broken stones. Coming toward her on the road was a large American military truck loaded with stacks of German weapons.

"Come on, Killer. You may have to protect me again, but you and I are going to Liège! Stop, stop," she called, and moved a few steps into the road waving her arms.

15

A PRISONER

Whe the American sergeant shoved Kurt into the watchtower with a gun barrel, Kurt felt it was all over. After a few brief questions in English to which Kurt responded with a puzzled shrug, the sergeant turned to the guard.

"Go git Cap'n Foster," he ordered. "He can ask this German in his own lingo what he's doin' wanderin' down this bridge in the dead a night."

The guard quickly ducked out the door. Holding a pistol on Kurt, the sergeant searched him with one hand. Kurt's clothes dripped steadily on the floor, forming small puddles and rivulets under his muddy boots. Soon the door opened again, and the guard ushered in a slim black officer who was buttoning his uniform blouse sleepily.

"What you got here, Sergeant?" the officer asked crossly. "Can't this wait until morning?"

"Sorry, sir. We can't git nuthin' outta this prisoner, and it's kinda unusual to find one on the bridge now. Every soldier assigned to blow the bridge either run off or already got captured. Thought maybe you'd like to ask a few questions. We've been warned Zkorzeny's frogmen were gonna try wreckin' our pontoon bridge, and I ain't takin' no chances. We need that pontoon bridge!"

Captain Foster looked at Kurt sharply and then in heavily accented German asked who he was and what his business was on the bridge.

"Kurt Müller, rank of private, 714804," Kurt replied.

"Yes, yes," the captain said wearily in German. "It is of the utmost seriousness. I must know your business on this bridge. Try again."

"Kurt Müller, rank of private, 714804," Kurt repeated, with a click of his heels. He continued to hold his arms up, hands linked together on top of his head.

"Put your arms down, Müller," Foster ordered. "You're getting everything wet. How long have you been out there, and what are you doing here?"

"Kurt Müller—"

"I know, I know." Captain Foster stared at him for several long moments. "How old are you, son? Are you any older than fifteen?"

Kurt shook his head.

"I thought not. Have you been hiding out somewhere and decided finally to make a break for it?" Kurt looked at the floor. The captain's tone was not unkind. He turned to the sergeant.

"Kids! They sent kids and old men to finish their bloody battles. Guard! Take this prisoner out to the prison compound, but give him some GI clothes first."

Captain Foster studied Kurt again. "Go with the guard,

Müller. He will give you some dry clothes." The officer turned to leave, then on a sudden impulse said, "Are you hungry?" and when Kurt nodded, he added, "Give him some K-rations also, guard. I'll interrogate him again in the morning if I have time."

The captain looked at the sergeant and held out both hands, palms up, in a questioning shrug. "What are we going to do with all these prisoners? The Allies have taken over fifty thousand German prisoners in the last two weeks!"

The sergeant waved the guard and the prisoner out.

Kurt followed the soldier in the gray half-light of early morning. A drowsy supply sergeant issued a blanket and a change of clothes. Then the guard led Kurt down a path and into a cement house. The house was empty of furniture. Sleeping men rolled in their blankets lined the floor.

All prisoners, Kurt realized. After he discarded his wet clothes for the American work uniform, he ate dry rations from the small box the guard had thrust into his hand. Kurt looked around at the sleeping men.

He searched for a familiar faces among the twenty German soldiers on the floor. No one from his own company. *By now, they're dead.* He felt so alone. *If only Martin* — He rolled up in the blanket and was asleep before he had time for another thought.

A few hours later one of the prisoners shook him awake. "Get dressed," the man said. "They come to march us to eat in five minutes. Everyone must go. That's one of the rules. Roll your blanket first, but hurry."

Kurt turned eagerly. "What company are you from? Are there any prisoners here from the demolition company that was wiring the Remagen Bridge?"

The man put his fingers to his lips and shook his head. Evidently the Allies did not like the prisoners to communicate too much.

Kurt marched silently with the others to breakfast. He resolved to keep his eyes open for any of the men from his own unit. He couldn't help thinking about Rachel. How far had she gotten on her desperate journey? Had she forgotten him as soon as they were separated? He hoped nothing had happened to her. Or to Fritz.

Days began to stretch before him in a dull, unchanging routine, and he despaired of ever being free again. As a prisoner, however, Kurt did not feel ill treated. He and the fifty or so Germans in the two-story house were marched to and from a field mess hall three times a day, although often the meals consisted of dry rations. He noticed the Americans ate the same food.

A few days after Kurt's capture, Captain Foster gathered the prisoners together.

"Men, the war is almost over. The Allied forces are marching toward Berlin even now." As the prisoners exchanged skeptical glances, he continued. "This is not propaganda, and at any rate, the war is over for you. I do not know where you will be sent. Some prisoners have already been moved back to your concentration camps, which are now under our control."

Kurt wondered if Captain Bratge and the men of the demolition company could possibly be among them.

"As for the rest of you," the captain went on, "you will

merely have to wait. We can use you in our repairs of the Remagen Bridge. It has been severely damaged, and we still need it for the movement of troops and machines. Are there any volunteers before I *assign* some of you?"

The German prisoners sat morosely silent. Kurt looked around. *They haven't mistreated me,* he thought, *or shot me. Anything's better than waiting.* He stepped forward.

"I will work," he said. Only one other prisoner volunteered to aid with the bridge reconstruction.

"All right," Captain Foster said. "You two go with Lieutenant Overby here. He cannot speak German, but he will show you what to do."

Kurt and the other prisoner, not quite as young as Kurt, followed Lieutenant Overby to the bridge. Kurt's eyes searched the distant cliffs, but the hills were green and silent, without a break or clearing in the trees to show that any living being had ever penetrated their virgin wilderness.

The snow will be gone by now, and soon the wine cellar owner will return to the cave to test the wine or to move some of it to another cask. Surely someone will know we've been in the cave. Maybe from the ashes of our fire or the tap on one of the barrels. But the owner might think one of his workers left the tap last fall. He recalled that the door had been broken loose from its hinges and left standing against the cave wall. *Maybe the cave owner is dead and won't ever return. By now,* he thought gloomily, *the American soldiers have drunk all the wine.* Then he remembered their initials and grinned to himself. *How the finder will puzzle over that!*

The lieutenant indicated to the two Germans that they were to help move a heavy metal plate to an almost-severed arch of the bridge. Kurt and his companion went with the American soldiers to take the plate to the center of the bridge. As they lifted the large, unwieldy disk, there was a sudden explosion near them. Water flew skyward as a shell exploded under the already weakened structure.

Kurt and the other prisoner dived into a nearby ditch with the American soldiers. They lay there for what seemed hours as shells rained about their heads. The prisoner, a young soldier named Gustav, explained the shells to Kurt.

"That is the Karl Howitzer, a 132-ton monster. It fires a shell of over 2,000 kilos. The Germans will destroy the bridge now," he said confidently. "It's a tank-mounted gun. I think our men are firing from about fifteen kilometers to the west," he added, pointing.

Kurt, who saw quite a scattered pattern to the shells, doubted whether the howitzer was doing much damage to the bridge. The shells continued to drop haphazardly. One hit a house about 250 meters to the east. Kurt was sure the house was occupied. He had noticed people going in and out a number of times as he had been marched to the mess hall.

The lieutenant finally ordered the men to leave the plate where it was. The prisoners did not understand the command but comprehended the officer's impatient gesture toward their quarters.

Kurt suspected the American soldiers didn't care much for Lieutenant Overby. He was a bantam rooster of a man who wore his shiny gold bars on his epaulets and collar even though this was frontline fighting. Kurt and his fellow soldiers had been told to shoot at officers before enlisted men; thus Overby's pride increased his chances of a sudden death. Kurt supposed the man's diminutive size caused him to strut and shout as he did.

As the prisoners walked back to the house where they were billeted, Kurt asked Gustav the question which was on all the prisoners' minds.

"When do you think we'll be sent back to a prisoner-of-war camp?"

"Soon, I hope," Gustav told him. "I don't want to get killed at this bridge." His expressed burning desire was to "get the hell out of this war and go home to my farm near Munich."

Kurt hoped he wouldn't be among those sent back. *The camp won't be near Liège*, he thought. *Where will it be?*

16

DEATH OF A BRIDGE

*A*fter mess call the next morning, Lieutenant
Overby rounded up his work crew and sent for
the two German prisoners. Kurt looked at Gustav as they
climbed the pathway to the bridge from the house where
they were quartered.

"Did you really think that howitzer was going to get the
bridge?" Kurt asked. "It's still standing. I don't think we
can kill that bridge or win the war!"

Gustav spat on the ground ahead of them. "We may
have lost the war, but we have not lost our farms," he
said. "The land is still there. I do not believe the enemy
will occupy our farms."

"What do you mean our land is still there? Everything
my family had, our house, our barn, was blown up!" He
stared at Gustav.

"Where was your farm?"

"Leipzig. Near the aircraft plant." Kurt walked along
looking at the ground rather than Gustav. Sometimes he
had to choke back tears when he thought of what might
have happened after he left the farm.

"Oh. Your family?"

"I don't know. I heard they got away, but that's all I know."

Hands in his pockets, Gustav's pointed weasel-like face evaluated the answers. "A farm is never gone," he said shrewdly. "You must know that."

"No, I don't know that! What do you mean? I know all our buildings were destroyed. Even our stock and my dog were killed. My mother and father and my sister Katzi were at church when it happened. Otherwise they would be gone too! What are you saying — it's never gone?"

Gustav prodded Kurt in the ribs with his elbow. "After the war is declared over, you can go back and search for your family. If you find them, good. If you don't, you can go back and claim your land. Or sell it. If it were mine, I'd farm it. When I get back to Munich, I'll plant rutabagas, potatoes, sugar beets, maybe grain."

With a slant-eyed glance at Kurt, he added, "I plan to grow barley for the brewers. We'll come back. You'll see."

Privately, Kurt thought Gustav was a little crazy. *The farm, though, was worth thinking about. You can't blow up an entire farm; that's true. But I'll look for my family until I find them! Perhaps — no, it's better not to dream.*

Kurt and Gustav followed the lieutenant onto the bridge. Once again the workers, American and German, struggled with the heavy plate. They intended to lift it, then weld it to the arch so that the top of the bridge would not come apart. The plate would serve as a giant patch holding the two arches of the bridge together.

Kurt looked at the bridge. It had undergone a tremendous onslaught in the last two weeks. He knew that reverberations from American antiaircraft batteries and eight-inch howitzers as well as German shells had jolted the bridge. He thought that the blast from Sergeant Faust's original triggering of the emergency charge had probably weakened the structure more than anything. He remembered the huge hole that had appeared in the middle of the bridge after that explosion.

He trudged up to the place where the big metal plate had been dropped.

"Lift, lift," the command came, and the circle of workers with Kurt among them hefted the metal disk and carried it to the welders, who would attach it to the arch.

Suddenly there was the sound of a rifle-shot, no more than that. As the workers looked up in amazement, the upper arches of the great bridge began to collapse. The entire structure trembled, and dust rose from the wooden planking. Workers dropped their tools and dashed for the nearest bank.

With an almost-human shriek, the truss spans vibrated, separated, and sank slowly into the river. American soldiers who had not made it to shore plunged into the Rhine. For a brief horror-struck moment, Kurt watched bodies falling into the river. He remembered again Martin's unnecessary and terrible death.

Behind his feet, the span opened into a yawning chasm. He found himself standing on the edge of nowhere, at the crumbling border of disaster. Lieutenant Overby had slipped off the bridge, but as he fell, the panic-stricken officer had grabbed the edge of the planking with both hands. His body dangled from the bridge, legs waving in the air. In an automatic reaction, Kurt threw himself onto the remaining boards, reached down, and grasped the small man under the arms. As he did, Kurt felt someone hold his feet. This gave him more leverage to maintain his grip on the weight hanging from his arms.

He held on to the horrified officer. Beneath the American lieutenant, cement and steel crumbled and sank into the water. Kurt saw twenty or thirty heads bobbing around in the current. Their only hope was that someone would pull them out of the river at the treadway bridge, almost two kilometers downstream.

Kurt held on with all his young strength to the gasping man. *It's now or never. If he goes, I go with him!* With this thought and all the power he could summon, he yanked the American officer up onto the planking as if Overby were a full feed sack on his father's farm. Then he and Gustav, who had thrown himself on Kurt's lower legs and feet to anchor him, began dragging the almost-unconscious man to safety on the west bank. Their bodies sensed the earthquakelike tremors as the bridge crumbled and broke away under them. Kurt felt as if he were running uphill. The last section of bridge between them and the bank was slanting and breaking away.

Gustav pointed ahead with his free hand and shouted, "We'll never make it. Let him go!"

"No!"

The two prisoners struggled on, hauling Overby between them.

At the edge many hands, beckoning and pleading for more speed, reached for the desperate, gasping pair with their heavy burden. Kurt's chest felt as if it were bursting. His arms were almost pulled from their sockets. Huge chunks of cement and steel fell from under their running feet into the river.

As they neared the American soldiers on the bank, Kurt held out his right hand in a final lunge for safety and grasped another man's hand. As the three men were jerked onto the bank, the planking they had crossed dropped into the Rhine.

Gasping and choking for breath, Kurt lay with his face on the ground. His arms and legs trembled violently. Lying beside him, Gustav fought for breath also.

The shaking in his body finally eased, and Kurt sat up. With many back-slappings, the Americans helped the two young German prisoners up and hauled the shaken, white-faced Overby to his feet. The little officer held out his hand in turn to each of the prisoners. They could not understand his words, but they knew what he meant.

The bridge was gone. Kurt looked back at the wreckage. This link between the east and west bank of the Rhine River no longer existed. He and Gustav were dismissed, and they walked wearily back to the mess hall.

What will the Americans do with us now? Kurt wondered. *They don't need us to work on their own bridges. The Remagen Bridge is gone. They will take all the prisoners and leave.*

17

FREE

*I*n the morning American military trucks drew up to the prison compound and loaded the men to take them to prisoner-of-war camps. Kurt and Gustav waited with the others, but when they stepped forward to climb into a truck, the sergeant in charge pushed them back. He said something in English which they did not understand.

They looked at each other. Gustav shrugged. "They're saving us for better things? A reward?"

Kurt was not so sure. "They need workers, maybe."

The two filed back into the village house. It was a desolate scene. Kurt kicked at the blankets that littered the floor. "What do they have in mind for us?" he asked aloud. He did not voice his fears. It was frightening to be singled out, to be kept behind. No matter where the other men were being taken, at least they were together.

"I don't know what they want with us," Gustav answered, "but whatever it is, I will escape one way or another. The war's almost over, and I'm going back to my farm even if I have to hide in alleys and eat out of garbage cans till I get there!"

After the trucks were loaded, the sergeant came into the house looking for Kurt and Gustav. He motioned to them, and they followed him silently up the trail to command headquarters. Inside, the sergeant waved them to chairs by a closed door. He knocked twice and opened the door as a voice called from within. He spoke briefly in English, then indicated the two young Germans should go in.

As they entered the office, Captain Foster and Lieutenant Overby broke off their conversation. Overby shook hands with both prisoners and made a short formal announcement in English. He concluded with a question. The boys looked inquiringly at Captain Foster.

The captain explained in German. "Lieutenant Overby wants to thank you for your brave actions of yesterday, and he asks if there is any way he can help you. The two of you obviously saved his life at considerable risk to your own."

Gustav was the first to respond. With narrowed eyes he asked, "What can he do for us? Can he give us our freedom?"

Captain Foster spoke to the lieutenant briefly. When Kurt saw the lieutenant nod, his heart jumped.

Then Foster said, "We are running out of places to keep prisoners. Soon the war will be over, and the official order will be given to free most of them. But both of you can leave now. Where will you go?" He looked at Kurt as he spoke.

Kurt stammered slightly as he answered. He could hardly grasp his luck. "To—to Liège, sir. I would attempt to find my way to Liège. I cannot search for my family in Germany until I can move about the country freely. I think it is a little early for that, sir. When the war is declared over, I will return."

Captain Foster nodded in understanding. "You are probably right. It is a little premature to go wandering around Germany."

"Let me go and you will not have to worry about where." Gustav stood first on one foot and then on the other. "Now? May I leave now?"

"Yes." Captain Foster stood. "You understand this is somewhat unofficial, but I will see to it that neither of you is detained in any way." Then he spoke to Kurt. "Private Müller, we have a truck going back to Liège this afternoon for R and R—rest and recreation—for some of our men who have not had a leave in a long time. If you will wait outside the mess hall area, I will tell Sergeant Turner to make room for one more."

There was a pause while Captain Foster explained the situation to Lieutenant Overby in English. Then the two officers shook hands with the young soldiers. "Good luck," they said.

"Danke, danke," the boys replied with wide smiles.

Captain Foster ushered them out and spoke to the waiting sergeant briefly in English. The sergeant saluted and left.

Kurt and Gustav walked outside. Kurt thought the sun on his face had never before felt so good. He and Gustav pounded each other on the back. "Auf Wiedersehen." Gustav waved and was off, striding like a man late for an appointment.

Kurt walked quickly to the mess hall and sat down on

the grass to wait for the truck. A small group of American soldiers sat there also. There was a great deal of laughter and horseplay among the soldiers as they waited. Kurt observed several of them counting their money. He wondered what he would do without any.

His happiness was almost suffocating. Then suddenly: *What if she never got there?* he thought. *So many things could have happened.* He waited for the truck with a mixture of dread and excitement.

18

LE CAFÉ MEUSE

*T*he truck arrived soon after noon, and a sergeant leaped from the passenger's side to read the names off a roster. As he read from his clipboard, the men showed him their passes and jumped into the truck to sit on narrow benches lining the sides. Another bench ran down the center.

"Benson, Garibaldi, Isaacson, Lampi . . ." Soon he had checked off all the names. The truck seemed filled to capacity. He reached for the rear gate to close the lower half of the truck's back end. Kurt stood waiting nervously. He stepped forward.

"Bitte?"

The sergeant looked at him closely. "Oh, you're Müller."

Kurt nodded when he heard his name. "Then get in there and be quick about it." The sergeant pointed to the truck. Kurt stepped up into the back. The men squeezed down to make room for him. One or two gave him puzzled glances, but no one said anything directly to him.

The sergeant raised the gate and secured it. The driver

shifted gears, and the truck chugged slowly down the rutted side road toward the main road. Kurt stared at the road sign. LIÈGE, 60 KM. *Had she also looked at that sign?*

As the vehicle moved toward Liège, the truck bed rattled and shook its crowded passengers without mercy. Clearly anticipating their holiday from war, the soldiers laughed and joked as they rode. The truck pulled up a few hours later at an old hotel in the center of town and emptied its boisterous riders at the front door.

Kurt walked slowly down the sidewalk of the crowded city street. An aura of springtime and excitement filled the air even though there was destruction everywhere. Kurt supposed the news of the Allies reaching Berlin would have caused the air of celebration here. He had not been as skeptical as some of the other prisoners when Captain Foster had announced the Allies' triumph.

The streets had evidently been cleared of rubble, and many American Army vehicles moved rapidly through them. American soldiers walked arm and arm with Belgian girls. At the end of the block, a fountain in a little park spewed crystal droplets high in the air while an American soldier embraced a pretty girl on a park bench.

As he walked, Kurt noticed his reflection in the darkened glass of a store window. For an instant, he wondered who it was. He supposed bystanders would think he was an American soldier because of his fatigues, the uniform work clothes issued to all the prisoners and worn also by the Americans for work details. He ran his fingers through his hair. *Longer now. Makes me look older*, he thought.

He felt older. Only a few months had passed since the fifteen-year-old farm boy had been drafted into the German Army. He had kissed his mother, made promises to Katzi—promises he couldn't keep. He had seen the war, witnessed men wounded and killed, felt his country crumble around him. Life would never be the same again.

Here in this place of safety, new hope unfolded like the glossy petals of the red tulips beginning to bloom in the park. *I'll go to Rachel, and she'll be all right*, he told himself. *When it's safe to return to Germany, I'll find my family.* Yet he was afraid.

He felt alone and lost. Without money, his only means of finding Le Café Meuse was on foot, but which was the way? He was not used to big cities. He heard people speaking in several different languages as busy groups passed him. He recognized French, even though he could not understand it, and a language that might be Flemish. He knew that Belgium was a country of at least three languages. He stopped several busy shoppers before he found one who spoke German and would take the time to answer his question. An old lady dressed entirely in black nodded her head vigorously.

"It is far, yes, but not too far to walk. Go down this street until it turns to the right. You must leave the street there and go left. Do you understand? Do not follow this street beyond the turn."

Kurt nodded. "And after I turn left?"

"You can see the River Meuse, and you will immediately come upon Le Café Meuse a few blocks from the banks of the river. You will recognize it by a blue-and-white striped awning in the front. It is small but a very good cafe. I once ate a delicious meal of escargot — well, you do not want to know what I ate." The old lady shook her cane at Kurt. "You understand where it is, no?"

Kurt assured her that he did. "Danke, danke."

Now that he had a direction in mind, he walked briskly. Bicyclists passed him by the hundreds, riders of every age. He walked by shops that were only a blur of color to him. The entire city seemed to be celebrating spring.

He hurried on, his excitement almost unbearable. He stopped at an intersection. A blue-coated policeman was directing traffic with a whistle. Kurt waited with a small group of people — babies in carriages who were red faced from the cool spring breeze, their round, smiling mothers, and black-clad old women. *Is everyone smiling or is it my imagination?*

The whistle shrilled and a white-gloved hand waved the pedestrians briskly across in front of the impatient traffic. A large bus ground gears and rumbled down the street, leaving a cloud of gray smoke behind it. Kurt paused on the opposite corner. The river. Yes, he could see the river. He walked toward it. He watched anxiously on both sides of the street for the cafe.

A bakery, an apartment house, a cobbler's shop, a small grocery, a bar, and a harness shop. A blue-and-white striped awning down the street caught his eye. The sun shone on the sign above it. *Le Café Meuse.* He crossed the street and walked down the sidewalk toward the cafe. He went up a short flight of steps into the restaurant.

Once inside, he examined the cafe curiously. In a sun-lit corner by a back window, two old men played dominoes on a battered wooden table, pausing occasionally to write the score on a scrap of paper. Voices emanating from the kitchen had an odd, lilting cadence that sounded to him more like French than German, although he could not actually make out the words.

He hadn't thought much about the language problem. Rachel spoke perfect German, but then she had left Belgium for Germany at the age of two. Would these people understand him? *Surely,* he thought, *in a country so close to Germany, some people speak both languages.*

In the center of the room, two old ladies bent their blue-gray heads together over a teapot. Each whispered rapidly, hardly waiting for the other to finish before beginning again. The lone waiter approached Kurt. The man examined Kurt's American uniform, then spoke to him briefly in English.

"Bitte?" Kurt stammered. "Sprechen sie Deutch? (Do you speak German?) I am looking for Rachel Gildemeister. Do you know her? Is she here?"

The waiter's face closed and hardened. "No," he answered in heavily accented German. "I do not know her. Do you wish to be served?" He indicated a nearby table.

"Isn't this Le Café Meuse?" Kurt asked, searching for the name on the door, a matchbox, anywhere.

The waiter nodded and pulled out a chair for Kurt.

But he couldn't sit down and order a meal. He had no money. This wasn't the way he had imagined it would be at all. *She had to be here!* He tried to remember what Rachel had told him about the restaurant. He knew the man's name; surely he could remember it now when he needed it.

"Poppo? Do they call you Poppo?"

Fleeting expressions of recognition and alarm crossed the man's face. Then he called rapidly in French to someone in the kitchen. After a brief silence, a strident answer returned — also in French — from the cook, evidently.

The waiter looked stern. And watchful, it seemed to Kurt. "We do not know of any Rachel Gildemeister. I am sorry."

Kurt stood bewildered for a few seconds. He had not thought beyond this moment. He had been so sure he would find Rachel here. Somehow he had hoped her relatives might give him a place of refuge until the war ended. Then he could return to Germany to look for his family. Now he didn't know which way to turn. Although it was foreign to his nature, he felt he should argue with the waiter, perhaps even threaten him.

"Danke," was all he muttered in answer to the waiter, who might or might not be Poppo, but the man had already disappeared into the kitchen.

Slowly Kurt left the cafe. He stood on the sidewalk and studied the restaurant sign. *Le Café Meuse.* Why hadn't he paid better attention to Rachel when she spoke of the cafe! He half turned to go back into the place. What was the use? If they didn't know her, she had never gotten this far. And if they were lying to him, it amounted to the same thing. No Rachel.

He walked down the sidewalk from the cafe. *Where could he go? What could have happened to her?*

He looked at the people passing by — the red-faced

babies sleeping in carriages, their smiling mothers, the policeman blowing his whistle in the distance. Nothing had changed. Everything had changed. He no longer perceived the crowds as happy and laughing. Some of them must feel as desperate as he did.

A plan of action eluded him. Should he return to the hotel and ask to go back with the American soldiers after their weekend in Liège? And where would he wait until they were ready to return? He had no money for a room. *Perhaps a park bench* —

He rejected the idea instantly. The soldiers would probably not go back to the same camp near the Remagen Bridge after their short leave. All the prisoners had been transferred. He had no idea where they had been taken. And whoever heard of a released prisoner asking to be taken back?

Captain Foster had told Gustav and him that the Americans were running out of places to keep prisoners and soon would free them all. It was useless to go back.

He began walking aimlessly as his mind shuffled possibilities, then discarded them. He could have gone with Gustav. Actually, that thought had crossed his mind during the talk with Captain Foster and Lieutenant Overby. Kurt had been afraid that Gustav was the kind of person who could easily exist on the land, to whom stealing food or money was a necessary evil. He probably would not consider it immoral or illegal. Kurt didn't think he could travel across Germany stealing from people. What was left?

There was only one thing he knew well — farming. How could that work to his advantage now? He looked around and realized his wandering had not been as aimless as he thought. Subconsciously his feet had begun taking him out of the city, away from the traffic and noise. The River Meuse was on his left. His direction would be toward the country. He would find a farm, he decided. *Then what? I will request a job for a few weeks.* His stride became purposeful as he left the shops and wide city streets behind.

19

ROCK POTATOES

*S*oon Kurt found himself where the houses were few. In the distance he saw dust rising from a field. He walked quickly now. Before he reached the field, a man came out of a nearby house and walked to his barn. Kurt knocked tentatively on the barn door so as not to startle the farmer. The man was lifting harnesses from a peg on the wall as Kurt entered.

"Here, you! Get off my property," the man bellowed. "I don't want no American deserter around here. I don't want no trouble with the American Army!"

"Sir," Kurt said softly. "I am looking for work — temporary work for a few weeks only. Do you — "

The farmer picked up a pitchfork and started for Kurt. The boy ran as far as the road, and when no one came after him, slowed his pace. His breathing was ragged for a few minutes until he realized he was not in danger. He continued to march toward the same distant field.

The sun had set in the west by the time Kurt reached the field. As he did, he understood the cloud of dust. A man was plowing with a team of horses and walking behind it just as Kurt and his father did, but one of the horses was half wild. The furrows behind the plow wavered here and there. The farmer swore steadily at the right-hand horse, which seemed unable to settle down to the job.

Young, Kurt decided, *and this is the first time the owner's had him in the fields.* The other horse plodded along steadily. Kurt climbed over the fence and hurried around behind the plow. He caught the colt by the bridle and held on firmly down the full length of the field.

After a startled "Hey, you! What are you doing?" at first, the farmer nodded in understanding and allowed Kurt to walk beside the team up and down the field. Finally the farmer pulled the horses to a halt and began to unhitch the plow near the fence.

"You know horses, do you, boy?" the old man asked.

"Yes, sir. Whenever we started a new horse in the fields, either my dad or I walked with him at first until he got the idea of working with another horse in a team." Kurt was relieved to find that the old man spoke German.

The farmer began leading the horses down the road to his barn. He cast a puzzled glance at the boy's uniform.

"It's all right," Kurt explained. "I'm — I'm German, but I can't go home till the war's over. These American fatigues are clothes somebody gave me. Do you — do you have any temporary field work for me?"

"Got no money to pay, son. Thanks for today, though."

Kurt ducked his head in acknowledgment of the gratitude and stood in the road as the man led the horses toward the barn. The sky had dulled to a soft purple and the sun was down. *Where would he go? Even the cave had been better than an open field.*

"Wait!" The farmer called back to him. "How are you at milking?"

Kurt turned eagerly. "We milked twelve!"

"Tell you what. Come along with me and do m'evening milking. We can give you your keep for a while."

Kurt followed him to the barn. After instructions and a brief introduction, the old man went to the house and left Kurt to feed and water the horses and milk six Jersey cows.

The boy led the horses into their stalls and hung their harnesses on pegs. After he fed and watered them, he searched for the necessary pails and a stool for the milking. Old Pieter, the farmer, kept his equipment in the same general places in the barn as Kurt's father had. When he finished, Kurt walked hesitantly to the back door of the house, set down his pails, and knocked.

"So the old fellow got someone to do his milking." The woman who answered the door laughed. "Pieter has always hated milking. Set the pails in the dairy there, that door to your left, and wash up at the pump. Supper's almost ready. Kurt, is it?"

"Yes, ma'am."

"I'm Lissette. Get a move on, now. Pieter's been working since sunup with that new colt and he's hungry as a bear coming out of hibernation!"

Kurt used the outhouse, cleaned up at the pump, and hurried in to supper.

In bed that night, he tried to sort out his impressions of the old couple and their farm. The house, barn, and animals made him feel at home, yet there was a strange dreamlike quality about being there. Lissette had put him in a bedroom which smelled moldy, as if it had been closed up and not heated for many months. It had clearly been a boy's room. Long skis stood in the corner. A soccer ball sat on the dresser. There were no clothes in the closet.

Perhaps it had been their son's room. He was afraid to ask. Maybe the boy had been killed in the war. There were several pictures of a boy on the dresser. And the old couple — they weren't really old; perhaps not much older than his parents. Something had happened to make them old before their time. He fell asleep, still puzzling over the incident in Le Café Meuse. Had the waiter been afraid of him for some reason?

At daybreak, Lissette called to Kurt. The following days became a chain of hard work punctuated by huge meals of boiled potatoes, sauerkraut, sausage, rutabagas, and occasionally a dessert of Apfelstrudel. Lissette was pleased by Kurt's appetite. He remembered Martin's bragging about his wife Anna's Strudel. He finally told Pieter and Lissette about Martin, his own escape, and the cave. Neither of them could understand what had happened in the cafe when he asked for Rachel.

"Try again," Lissette kept telling him. But Kurt knew it would only be another disappointment.

A week went by, then two. He wondered about the war. Pieter listened to an old radio each night after supper, but for weeks there was no news other than that of the Allies marching into Berlin. Finally one evening early in May, as Kurt started upstairs to bed, Pieter jumped out of his chair and began to waltz the amazed Lissette around the living room.

"Papa! What has gotten into you?"

"Didn't you hear the announcer? Tomorrow is May eighth, is it not?" Pieter shouted.

"Yes, you know it is." Lissette was out of breath from whirling.

"May eighth has been declared Victory in Europe Day by the Allied forces! The war is over!" He hummed "Lili Marlene" as he danced Lissette around.

"I'll be leaving tomorrow, then," Kurt said happily. "I can go home and look for my parents!"

Suddenly Lissette burst into tears. Pieter stopped dancing and held her as she cried. "If it had only ended sooner, Papa. A year sooner."

"I know." Pieter comforted her, holding her tightly. "Try to be glad for the world that it is over."

Kurt climbed the steps slowly. *So they had lost someone.* He picked up a framed black-and-white photo from the dresser in his room. The laughing face of a boy not much older than he looked back at him. Kurt was thankful the war was over, but for many, it hadn't come soon enough. He prayed he would find his father and mother and his sister Katzi safe and sound.

I will look for them, he vowed, *until I find them. Then we will start over on our farm.* But what about Rachel? Wherever she was, did she know the terrible war was finished at last?

In the morning, he did the milking for the last time, then thanked Pieter and Lissette for taking him in. Pieter insisted on giving him a few marks.

"You can't go into town without money to celebrate," he said. "Go find that girl you told us about!"

Kurt waved good-bye. When he was down the road about half a mile, he turned to see their house. Smoke rose from the chimney; Lissette was making another good meal. Pieter was working in the field with the two horses who now pulled together steadily. Kurt smiled and set out for Liège at a brisk pace. He planned to hitch-hike, if he could, out of Liège into Germany to Leipzig.

It was useless to look for Rachel again. He hesitated when he realized he had followed the river back to the street where the cafe stood. *It's hopeless,* he thought. But his feet carried him toward the cafe. The street looked the same — mothers pushing baby carriages, delivery boys riding bicycles, and everyone laughing and chattering happily. Huge banners above the wide streets proclaimed in French, German, and English that the war was over. He crossed the street and stood on the cafe's sidewalk. He studied the sign. *Should he go in? Why bother?*

He glanced at the back stoop as the cook emptied something into the garbage pail. A dark red plume of a tail showed at the edge of the building. It wasn't! It couldn't be!

"Fritz!" Kurt yelled. "Fritz, come here!"

The tail withdrew. Then the dog bounded around the corner. When he recognized Kurt, he hurled himself on the boy with a series of excited yelps. On his hind legs, he was almost tall enough to lick Kurt's face. His tail was a whirling fan of love.

"Fritz, down! What are you doing?" A girl dressed in a blue waitress's uniform with a blue-and-white striped apron hurried down the restaurant steps. Kurt knelt by the dog, hugging him close. He looked up and saw Rachel. He was unable to speak. Her hair was combed smoothly back and fastened with a blue ribbon behind her neck. Tiny gold earrings glittered in her earlobes.

She looks so different! She's a stranger. He didn't know this beautiful girl. Had he ever been a part of her life? It seemed impossible now.

"Kurt! Is it really you?" Rachel stared in surprise. "In an American uniform?"

He stood slowly and smiled at her self-consciously. What did he and this lovely girl have in common? In the cave it had been different. They had both been cold and hungry and were trying to survive. He was embarrassed that he had come here, but he couldn't stop smiling at her.

She moved as close to him as she could with Fritz wagging frantically between them. Sunlight glinted through the huge tree branches overhead and dappled the busy city sidewalk under their feet. A boy pushing a cart filled with bread for the market wheeled around them. Two mothers with baby carriages separated as they approached the soldier and the waitress who stood looking at each other as if they were alone. The women joined each other again without missing a syllable of their conversation.

"Was it you who came looking for me?" Rachel asked him in amazement. "They said some man."

"Yes. Didn't they tell you?"

"Kurt! You didn't even tell them who you were! They were afraid to talk to you. All Poppo said was that an American soldier who spoke perfect German wanted to find me. They were protecting me. They would have recognized your name. I was at the market that day or you would have found me here working." She stood looking at him with an odd expression. "Somehow you don't look like a boy anymore. That's why they didn't think it might be the friend I told them about."

Kurt smiled at her and ran his hand self-consciously through his hair. "My hair's longer," he said, "and I do feel older. It doesn't matter. We're both safe now."

"I found my aunt and grandmother," Rachel said softly. "Now that the war is over, you can go back and look for your family—after you stay with us for a little while and tell me everything that's happened to you!" She reached for his hand and holding it tightly, urged him toward the cafe door. She looked up at him mischievously. "There's a special on tonight. It's rock potatoes, and I'll cook them for you myself."

Kurt smiled down at Rachel. This was definitely the girl he remembered. "I never thought we could do it, but we did, Rachel," he exulted. "We made it across the bridge to freedom!"

The cafe door closed behind the German boy, the Jewish girl, and a dog named Fritz, who were safe from war at last.